BLOODY GOLD

BLOODY GOLD

Chet Cunningham

Chivers Press ● G.K. Hall & Co.
Bath, Avon, England ● Thorndike, Maine USA

This Large Print edition is published by Chivers Press, England, and by G.K. Hall & Co., USA.

Published in 1995 in the U.K. by arrangement with the author.

Published in 1995 in the U.S. by arrangement with Chet Cunningham.

U.K. Hardcover ISBN 0–7451–2561–1 (Chivers Large Print)
U.S. Softcover   ISBN 0–7838–1239–6 (Nightingale Collection Edition)

The text of this Large Print edition is unabridged.
Other aspects of the book may vary from the original edition.

Set in 16 pt. New Times Roman.

Printed in Great Britain on acid-free paper.

British Library Cataloguing in Publication Data available

Library of Congress Cataloging-in-Publication Data

Cunningham, Chet.
  Bloody gold : Jim Steel / Chet Cunningham.
  p. cm.
  ISBN 0-7838-1239-6 (lg print : lsc)
  1. Large type books.   I. Title.   II. Title: Jim Steel.
[PS3553.U468B57   1975]
813'.54—dc20   94–47589

PROLOGUE

Jim Steel was a gold man. He didn't consciously try for the title. But more and more of those who lived beyond the Missouri River had heard of him and his exploits.

In the year of 1867 there were national heroes. In February of that year Nebraska was admitted to the Union as the thirty-seventh state, and the first ship passed through the Suez Canal half a world away; in March, the last French troops marched out of Mexico for good.

But Jim Steel was more interested in gold than in politics. It was true he had served as an elected sheriff for a time in Kansas, and later in Arizona. But law enforcement was not his forte. He was tried for murder twice while he was wearing a badge, but both times he defeated the charge. The affairs left such a bitter taste in his mouth that he gave up a career as a lawman.

Jim Steel began to think of gold. He put in an apprenticeship for a year in a hard rock mine, moved on through the silver country, and eventually discovered that gold didn't always have to come out of the ground ... not when it was secondhand.

Some called him a road agent, a rounder, but there were no wanted posters on him in any state or territory in the Union. Mid Pacific Railroad lost a shipment of gold from a sealed baggage car, and simply because Jim was on the same train he was suspected of it. But no evidence was ever found linking him with that missing twenty thousand dollars in gold.

In Abilene, Texas, a kissing bandit descended on a bank that had just taken a shipment of new twenty-dollar gold pieces. This lone bandit cleaned out over twelve thousand dollars worth of the loot and paused only long enough to kiss two pretty women customers as he left. Jim had been in the area and some said he did it, but again, no proof was brought out, and Jim wasn't saying 'yea' or 'nay' to the rumors.

Jim didn't mind the stories, he let them build and grow. His conscience was clear. He had paid his dues in the gold game, and now he was ready to get all of it he could.

The *Gold Wagon* adventure had been the result of a happy afterthought. Uncle Sam had decided to send a ton of gold from the mines of California to the mint in Washington, D.C. in 1866, and Jim just happened to find out about it, along with every other gold-hungry hooligan in the West. His try for the gold took an unexpected turn, but he did come up with some yellow for his trouble.

He had been shanghaied into the *Die of Gold* fracas. He was hired to help protect a five-man army party moving into the high Sierras at

Donner Pass, but it was a double cross and a frameup that became a personal affair, as Jim tried to save the U.S. Treasury Mint dies for the 1867 Double Eagle twenty-dollar gold pieces. Again some bars of free gold happened to wind up in his saddlebags as he rode for San Francisco.

Jim Steel wasn't the kind of a man who hunted trouble, but somehow it managed to find him. In a time when the average man stood five feet five inches tall, Jim was five eleven. Black hair partly covered his forehead and tangled with the collar of his black shirt. Jim usually dressed like a range hand: jeans, a flap-pocket shirt, and a low-crown gray hat with the brim curled on both sides.

Critics of Jim said he wasn't a real western hero at all. He'd rather kiss a pretty woman than his horse, they said, and in that small fact they certainly were right. But no petticoated filly had yet roped him for good, or kept him from moving on.

This time Jim Steel is in Arizona Territory in 1867, and that means Apache country. And he has the scent again, that sudden enthusiasm that is so familiar to anyone who has ever looked in his pan and found yellow, or studied an assay report and known for sure that it was … GOLD!

3

CHAPTER ONE

Jim Steel checked the distant outlines of the Dragoon Mountains as the rising sun streaked them with shadows. The previous evening he had pulled off the regular Tucson to Tombstone trail in search of some kind of shelter where he could spend the rest of the night. At last he had rolled up in his blankets under a thick spread of chaparral for a cold, dry camp.

Now he was eager to be on his way again. He packed the last of his breakfast things in his saddlebag and swung up on Hamlet, his big-boned, trusty buckskin. Jim looked forward to arriving in Tombstone, one of southern Arizona Territory's poor excuses for a town.

He sat high in the saddle, his left hand holding the reins. He had clear blue eyes that squinted now in the morning light, taking in everything around him as if he were a lead scout on a cavalry patrol. He stood an inch under six feet, and had thick black hair that crowded down on his forehead and hid both ears. Jim Steel wore a heavy black mustache and long sideburns to help protect his face from the desert sun. His skin had that look of a man who has spent more nights under the stars than under the blankets of a real bed. He rode well, and his lean body was tanned and hard as a weathered mesquite branch.

Now he let the buckskin pick his way through the spiny cactus and scattering of rocks, as he moved back to the main stagecoach trail. Jim sat the big horse patiently. He was long accustomed to Hamlet's habits and dislikes. He wasn't going to rush the animal. Trying to make time through this kind of chaparral and cactus was as smart as trying to out-jump a striking rattlesnake.

Hamlet lifted his head sharply, his ears pricked forward, a small nicker coming from his throat. Jim stopped the horse and listened. He heard nothing, then a neigh sounded to the left. Jim turned Hamlet toward it, curious who could be out in this country at this time of day.

Hamlet led him into a small wash Jim hadn't seen the night before, and then stopped suddenly. Ahead in a bend in the dry watercourse stood an Indian pony with no saddle, its rawhide hackamore and reins dragging the ground.

Just behind the horse lay the form of a man, an Indian, from what Jim could see. He moved up carefully, at a walk, and Hamlet tried to make horse-talk to the pony, which didn't respond. Jim was ten feet away when he realized the Indian was old and either very sick or dying. His wrinkled face showed many years of desert survival, and his arms and legs looked like little more than bones with brown skin stretched tightly over them.

6

Jim slid to the ground, dropped Hamlet's reins, and strode to the old man's side. The Indian gave no indication he heard Jim arrive.

'Honored grandfather,' Jim said in Spanish, hoping that this Apache spoke Spanish as many of them did, since they had lived in and out of Mexico and the U.S. for years. The man's eyes were closed, and Jim thought he might already be dead. But the horse was still there; it hadn't smelled death and run off.

Jim took the canteen from his saddle, knelt, and wet his hand. Then he pressed the dampness against the Indian's hot face.

'Old grandfather,' Jim said again, and this time the eyes flickered open, closed, and opened again for a moment before they faded shut. He was still alive.

Jim wet the Indian's face again, then lifted the frail old bones to a sitting position and wet his lips. The eyes came open once more and a rasping sound came from the old throat. Jim tipped the canteen to the Indian's lips to wet them. Now the man's tongue came out licking the water. Again Jim wet his lips. Twice more Jim went through the same routine, then he decided the dried out man was ready to drink.

The Indian coughed when he tried to take the water, but his eyes seemed more alert. Jim whistled for Hamlet to come and positioned him so the morning sun could not touch the tribal leader.

'Honored grandfather, you are far from

7

your Apache wickiup.'

The old head nodded slowly.

'You are not with a hunting party. Why are you here, so far from your own council fire?'

Jim offered him water again, and he took a small sip, then closed his eyes and swallowed. A smile spread over the sun-browned skin of his face, and he concentrated on talking.

'Life-song,' the old Chiricahua Apache said, his smile growing.

Now it made sense to Jim. The old man had been on his way to his favorite promontory, the highest peak he could still climb. No one would help him. He did not expect those from his tribe to help. Jim knew that if an adult Apache did not work, he did not eat. Everyone had to pull his weight with useful services. If you were sick or maimed or too old to work, you were put out. Jim had found more than one old squaw left by a trail to die, or shut out of her wickiup and sent into the desert to starve. Even young men so badly wounded in battle that they could no longer hunt or fight were left to die.

Now this old one was searching for his pinnacle where he would turn to the east and sing his life-song, a recollection of his proud moments, of his failures and his great victories and how well he had lived. It was a kind of last rite, a final confession, a cleansing of his soul. Jim had often heard of the ritual of the dying Apache, but he had never seen it.

He pressed the liquid to the parched lips

8

again and this time let the old Indian take a sip or two. As the realization came back to the Chiricahua that he had help, and that he now had a chance to sing his life-song, his body responded with amazing strength. But Jim knew the Indian would never ask a white-eye for help. If it were offered that would be another matter.

'Which is your promontory?' Jim asked.

The thin, ancient arm lifted slowly and pointed to the tallest mountain to the west, Apache Peak, almost eight thousand feet high, and fifteen miles away.

Jim shook his head. 'Your song will not last long enough for your bones to make that journey.'

The old man's nod was barely recognizable, then the tired face relaxed and seemed to smile. He had fooled the white-eye, had played a small joke on him. The old hand came up again and designated a small rise a hundred yards behind them, the highest land mass for two miles around.

Jim eyed the hump, then lifted the canteen again and permitted the dry throat a few more swallows of the fluid.

'What are you called?'

'Halcón Veloz,' he wheezed.

Jim saw the many scars on the battered old body.

'Swift Hawk has been a strong warrior for his people. I will help you to your high place.'

9

Before the Indian could reply, Jim put the canteen to his lips, letting him drink half a dozen sips. Then Jim picked up the withered form and carried him toward the outcropping of rocks on the small hill a hundred yards north. The old warrior had wasted away until he weighed no more than sixty pounds. The Chiricahua's eyes fastened in Jim's as he made the trip up the hill. The Indian never looked away from Jim as he walked around the rocks to the very top where the boulders lay. Jim stamped the grass and checked the rocks for early morning rattlers, then lowered Swift Hawk to the highest of the granite boulders.

The black eyes thanked Jim with dignity. 'You stay,' Swift Hawk said in Spanish, then he turned toward the east and raised both his arms.

The old Apache began his song, which came out as more of a chant on a five tone scale. In a quavering and weak voice Swift Hawk began to relive his life through the strengths and abilities of his dream animal, a giant hawk. At first he spoke in Spanish.

'O Great Life-giver, smile on me for I have soared high in life on outstretched wings to be in your favor. My wings have reached out for favorable winds to carry me over the trails of a hard life. I catch the gold rays of the sun on my feathers and reflect their warmth to my people. I fly so fast and so high that the arrows and bullets of my enemies cannot hit me.'

His voice quavered and died out. He went on speaking, but Jim couldn't hear him. The petition song continued for several minutes and at last became audible again.

'Now, I am ready to fly away into the heavens where the warm sun never sets, and where I can meet the Great Life-giver.'

The frail figure turned and beckoned Jim.

'It is done,' Swift Hawk said.

Jim lifted him and carried the Indian back to the wash. He found a spot where the mesquite offered a thin screen of shade. The sun would not find him until noon. Jim set Swift Hawk on the sand and brought his horse up nearby, then he offered the old man more water.

· Swift Hawk shook his head. 'In an hour my body will not need water. But now I must pay my debt to you. A Chiricahua has no more important debt than that he owes to one who helps him sing his life-song.'

Jim started to brush it aside, but saw the burning determination in the black eyes, so he sat crosslegged in front of the Indian.

'You know of squaw's clay?'

Without changing his expression, Jim nodded, but his interest leaped suddenly at the mention of squaw's clay, the soft rock good for nothing. White men called it ... gold.

'All white-eyes search for *oro*. You have heard of the sacred wall of gold in the Dragoon Mountains?'

Jim bobbed his head.

11

'Listen and watch closely. I will draw a map. You may go to the wall of gold once and leave with all the squaw's clay you can carry, but then you may never return again. All I can give you is the route, a map. You will have to be careful not to let the Chiricahua see you, for if they do they will kill you and dance around your bones.'

The ancient Indian leaned over and smoothed the sand with his hand. Then he began, using a broken cholla cactus stem as a marker.

'You know of Diablo Mountain, the tall peak in the Dragoons? Remember it well and come to it from the west side.' His hand worked quickly then, like a sand painter's, moving sand and making marks that showed peaks and ridges. When he was through he pointed to the mountains he had built.

'You know where the twin peaks of the *Ovejas* are, the Sheep's Horns?'

'I have heard of them.'

'They are here. Study the drawing well. Now memorize what is in the sand.' His finger traced the route again: past the tall mountain, through a pass, down a long valley, and then on to the twin peaks. 'This is the start, the first two days travel.'

'Old one, many have searched for the Apache wall of gold. Even most Chiricahuas don't know where it is. They say it's used only for secret rites of puberty for your young boys.

12

How can you know of this place?'

'I am subchief of the Chiricahua. Now only a few other Chiricahuas know of this place. Everyone who goes there for special occasions is sworn to secrecy.' He stopped suddenly and coughed. His voice faded again. 'Enough talk.'

He rubbed out the first map and smoothed the sand. Again Jim began memorizing names and routes. There was no indecision, no memory lapse. Each trail, each turn came quickly, clearly. The route went deeper into the Dragoons, near the stronghold where Cochise and his many followers lived, isolated now from the white-eyes. They were self-sufficient there, and the army had chosen to leave them alone.

Now the hand moved slower. Jim gave Swift Hawk another drink of water which he sucked at eagerly.

'The valley of three fingers, remember it. This is the key.' The Indian watched as Jim went over the route again and again, tracing the line with his finger. Jim's eyes met the Indian's black ones. Now he knew the secret, the map was his. Together they rubbed out the sand map.

Jim smiled, remembering what Swift Hawk had said about there not being any guarantee of safe passage. He was sure that Cochise and his three hundred warriors in the stronghold would do all they could to prevent his getting into the valley of gold. Since 1865 Cochise had grouped his followers in the Dragoons, and it was Chiricahua territory. Nobody in his right mind ventured even into the fringes of the area. The Dragoons were Chiricahua land, and hardly a rabbit moved or a tree fell that Cochise did not know about.

But the prospects of the fabled Apache wall of gold fascinated him. Now he knew a way in and out of the hidden valley to the wall of gold, where the story was that pure gold could be picked up in chunks the size of a saddle, or hacked out from a brilliant, gleaming, solid golden wall.

Swift Hawk looked at the canteen. His mouth was very dry again, but he would not ask the white-eye for *agua*. His voice was too weak to say the words, anyway. Jim lifted the canteen and placed it in the withered hands. The Chiricahua drank.

'*Gracias.*' He touched his head and looked at the sun through the branches. A white-hot light came burning at the center of his brain. He looked up at his promontory, then became still. His time was close at hand. The bridge was about to be broken, his wings folded...

'You must go, young friend. I wish to be alone now.' Swift Hawk spoke haltingly, in Spanish.

Jim saw that the old Indian was dying. He was at peace with himself and with the Life-giver. 'Goodbye, old grandfather Swift Hawk,' Jim said. Their eyes met for one last time, then

14

Jim turned and walked quickly to his horse and swung up. The Indian would be dead within an hour.

Jim moved Hamlet toward the trail, not looking back, leaving Swift Hawk his final moments in the dignity of privacy. But what about the map? For years he had heard about the famous Apache wall of gold in every mining camp from Tombstone to Sacramento. It was supposed to be twice as rich, twice as pure as gold from the Lost Adams Diggings. Did he really have the map to it burned into his memory? Or was it only the ramblings of a half-dead savage who was grateful?

A sudden urgency came over him. His business in Tombstone seemed less important now than it had an hour ago. Diablo Mountain, the Twin Sheep Horn Peaks, the valley with three fingers and the hidden valley. The names, the ideas kindled a flame in his mind.

When he came back to the stagecoach trail to Tombstone, Jim hesitated. That would only take him farther away from the start of Swift Hawk's map. He looked south along the trail, then turned north. He had by-passed Tucson when he came down the day before. Someone there might recognize him, and the delicate business deal he had working in Tombstone might be ruined. Now that didn't matter.

He was anxious to get back to the territorial town and fill his saddlebags with trail food:

beans, coffee, salt, jerky, soda crackers, maybe even some bacon, a loaf of bread and a can of peaches. Even then he would wind up living off the land for most of the trip. He wiped a spot of sweat off his forehead as the Arizona sun came down morning-hot. That is, he'd be living off the land if a Chiricahua brave didn't end his eating for all time.

The gold fever began burning into Jim's brain then. It was a malady he knew well. Not dust, not quartz rock gold, not even a nugget in a sluice box, but a wall of gold! Jim kicked Hamlet into a lope, anxious now to get to Tucson and get started into the Dragoons.

CHAPTER TWO

Jim Steel leaned wearily against the bar in Tucson's Gold Nugget Saloon and worked on his second beer. He had ridden into town an hour ago, and now the half-cooled suds washed the last of the trail dust from his throat.

He wanted to get fresh supplies and pack them on his saddle all ready for a quick ride. Jim hadn't decided if he would leave when it got dark and travel at night, or wait and go the first day into the Dragoons by sunlight. Whether or not he fell to the temptation of a hot bath and a soft bed at the Carriage House would decide his schedule. This was a one-man job, and he didn't want any hangers. As he rode into town he had seen one man who may have recognized him, but Jim hoped he hadn't. It had been five years. Jim was about to drink the last of his beer and get moving when a twenty dollar gold piece clattered next to him on the hard-topped bar.

'Bring the cowboy two more beers,' a deep, yet thin voice said beside him. There was the snap of command in the order, and when Jim turned he saw the blue coat of a pony soldier and a gleaming silver star on the man's shoulder. He almost snapped to attention as he stared at the general. The habits of two years were hard to break. He tensed, then reached for the rest of the beer and drained it.

'No thanks, soldier. I'm just leaving.'

A firm grip on Jim's arm slowed him, and the general's intense stare held him.

'Hear your name is Jim Steel. The one they call the Gold Man. That you're a slightly shady character with a nose for gold, and that you're said to be on speaking terms with that savage, Cochise.'

Jim took off his hat and scrubbed his hand over his forehead. That took care of his secret approach.

'Hear me out, cowboy. You've got nothing to lose. I'm looking for a man who knows the Chiricahua.'

Jim shrugged the hand off his arm. He saw the officer was keyed up, nervous, ready to shy

17

in the traces. Jim leaned back against the bar, and reached for one of the beers the apron brought. The general was old, he looked well over sixty.

Jim settled his hat back in its familiar groove. 'All right, soldier, what's on your mind?'

'I hear you can talk to Cochise. That you know him. Can you get me and my party through his scouts and into the stronghold?'

Jim put down the beer and wiped his black mustache with his shirt sleeve. 'I haven't seen Cochise for six years, but I think he'd remember me. Why?'

'Told you, consarn it! Need a good man to guide me into the stronghold. We'll take a five-man party and go in under a flag of truce.'

Jim scowled. He knew the army was leaving Cochise alone in the mountains. Now what the hell was this about? When he looked up the general was ahead of him.

'No, son. This isn't army business. I'm retired. It's strictly a private affair. No uniforms.'

'Private, with Cochise?'

'My daughter. A Chiricahua raiding band took a stage, looted it, killed the driver and guard, ran off the horses, and captured my youngest daughter. That was a week ago when she was heading East for school. She just turned eighteen.'

Jim watched moisture brim the old warrior's

18

eyes. The general looked all o   'Da gold
weathered and marked by the s
country. He seemed about five f
now his shoulders sagged, his be
forward and his jaw quivered whe
But the eyes were hard, and s ...,,, and
determined, with a snap and fire that mirrored
the strength of his will. Jim put down the beer
and turned toward the general.

'She's been gone a week. She's a woman, a
white woman. And she's the daughter of a
pony soldier general.' Jim shook his head.
'There isn't a chance in a thousand that she's
still alive.'

He looked the general in the eye. 'I'm sorry,
but there is absolutely no chance that your
daughter is still alive. Go back East to your
home and be glad you never found out exactly
what happened to the girl.'

Jim turned, not wanting to see any more of
the agony in the old face. He took another pull
at his beer.

'For God's sakes, man, she's just a girl. She's
only been gone for a week. If we get in there
fast under a flag of truce and offer Cochise
something he wants, like fifty head of prime
steers...'

He stopped and touched Jim's shoulder.
'Face me, mister, when I talk to you!' There
was a ring to the words, but there was the blight
of panic, too.

Jim turned.

mit, Steel. I'll give you two thousand in to lead us in there, no matter what we find. hat's more money than you could save in ten years punching cattle.'

'I'm not a cowboy ...' Jim pushed the hand away from him. 'And I don't particularly like generals. For two years some stupid generals ordered me around, and damn near got me killed three times.' Jim glared at the man. 'Did you serve around here?'

The old man nodded.

'You're not General Miles, that's for damn sure. West? Are you General Joseph West?'

The strained face in front of Jim nodded.

'Then you know the Chiricahua. You know their little tricks.' He paused. 'West, yeah ... it was your men who slaughtered Mangas Colorado, the great war chief of all the Apaches, when he was your official prisoner.'

General West sighed. 'The savage died as he attempted to escape. A military court cleared both me and my men.'

'Naturally, but did Cochise clear you? He is Mangas' son-in-law! And now they have the daughter of the man responsible for the death. I see your problem, General. You better pray those redskins didn't find out who she was.'

'Then you'll lead my party?' West asked, his face lighting with new hope.

Jim snorted. 'Not even if you were President Johnson himself asking me.'

'But my daughter...'

20

'She's dead. Accept that and learn to live with it. General, how many men have you watched die?'

The general brushed it aside.

'That's my little girl ... my Becky ... I remember when she was born. All that first year she was sickly.' His eyes blazed again. He turned, grabbed Jim's denim jacket, and pulled him forward. 'You've got to go, soldier. Get the hell out there and fight! That's an order. I don't put up with insubordination in the ranks.'

Jim fought back an urge to knock the man down. The general wasn't right in the head. He'd seen a corporal do the same thing during the siege of Petersburg. The man suddenly began screaming and raving, talking to his wife, seeing strange things in the sky. When the bombardment began he crawled into a hole and cried until the battle was over.

Tender fingers smoothed the old general's face. Jim saw it was a woman's hand, saw a fancy hat. He edged back and heard the voice.

'Father, it's all right. Hush now. Don't get so excited. It's going to be fine, Father, just fine. You'll see. Don't worry now. Come back to the hotel with me. We'll find Becky. I promise you we will.'

The general's hand relaxed on Jim's shirt and Jim moved backward a step. Beside the blue uniform stood a small and elegantly dressed woman. She wore a sleek, expensive

21

dress with flounces and lace that looked out of place in the roughness of the saloon. The hat with plumes almost hid her face, but she flashed a smile of appreciation at Jim as she led the general toward the bat-wing door.

'Sir?'

Jim turned. Standing at the bar near him was a foppishly dressed dude, a dandy straight from the streets of the East, and looking as out of place in the saloon as a fancy woman in a church.

'Sir, I deeply regret if my father has discomforted you in any manner. We are willing to make total and complete amends. He's not in the best of health, you see.'

'Forget it,' Jim said. He wanted to laugh at this sorry spectacle of a man. Instead Jim took another swig of the beer and pushed the empty mug down the bar to the apron.

'Sir. What you said about the savages. Are they really so mean and treacherous?'

Jim's dislike for the caricature of a man deepened. He was about twenty, sissified and strange. He reminded Jim of the half-man-half-woman he had seen in San Francisco.

'Damn right they're treacherous. Prisoners are considered the normal and legal spoils of an attack. The man who captures a prisoner has done so at considerable risk and danger to himself. So he owns her. He does with her as he pleases. Are you a part of the family?'

The youth rubbed a white hand over a nearly

22

beardless, pale face. Jim saw he was shocked, stunned by Jim's description of the Apaches.

'Look, just forget the girl, go back East where you belong. Your whole family will be better off.' Jim turned and walked out of the saloon.

He was approaching the hotel when the girl who had taken the general away stepped in front of him. He had to stop quickly to keep from bumping into her.

'Miss?' he said, touching his gray, low-crowned hat.

'Mr. Steel, did my father ask you to go find Becky?'

He smiled as he looked at her. She was small and pleasantly formed with a tiny waist, narrow shoulders, and a round face that now skittered between concern over her sister and amusement at his sudden discomfort.

'Yes, he asked me,' Jim said.

'Well, what did you tell him?'

'I said to forget about the idea. This is not Philadelphia, or Boston. We're not that civilized yet. After a week with the Chiricahuas she's either dead or ... well, worse than dead.'

'Sir, if you mean they have raped her, I expect that. So don't try to put me off by alluding to sexual intercourse. We both know that intercourse does not harm a woman. I've been married. Now, does she have a chance of surviving?'

Jim was so surprised by her frank talk that

he involuntarily took a step backward. She had not blushed, and her brown eyes held his firmly. Her features had locked into a severity that reminded him of her father. Her lashes were long, her well-formed nose was only a trifle too big for her face, and her lips seemed a shade too pink, as if they had just a little bit of help.

Jim took off his hat and rubbed his head. 'Oh, yes, ma'am, there's always a small chance she's alive. Her owner would use her, might keep her or sell her. His jealous squaws might kill her themselves. But I'd say there's maybe a ten percent chance she's still alive.'

'Then we must go in and bring her out.'

He shook his head. 'Impossible.'

'Nothing is impossible! Oh, no, nothing. Not if you wish to do something strongly enough.' She paused. 'Oh, excuse me, my manners are dreadful. My name is Mrs. Lawrence Edwards, Sarah West Edwards now. My husband died at the battle of Cold Harbor back in '64.'

So she really had been married. 'I'm sorry, ma'am.'

'Of course, so am I. Now, when do we start in for Becky? The sooner the better. Can we get going first thing in the morning?'

Jim Steel laughed. The thought of this small lady battling the Chiricahuas struck him as ridiculous. She stood no more than five feet tall and wouldn't weigh ninety-five pounds carrying a bucket of water.

24

'Don't laugh at me. I mean what I say. Besides, you haven't even told me your name yet.'

He told her.

'Jim, I see. All I heard was the Steel part. If you do know this Cochise, so much the better. We have a guide who has promised to lead us halfway into the stronghold. By that time we will attract the Indians' attention, and they'll see our white flag and lead us the rest of the way.'

'You've hired a guide, from here in Tucson?' Jim couldn't believe what she said. 'Somebody from this town will guide you into the Dragoon Mountains? How much are you paying him?'

'Two hundred dollars.'

Jim turned and studied a display of copper wash tubs in front of the general store. 'Lady, keep your money and use it to get tickets on the eastbound stage. Your guide will run out on you the first night and steal everything he can carry.'

'He seems perfectly honest to me.'

'Did he look ready to die? If he didn't, forget him, because any man who will guide you into the Dragoons must be ready to ride his last mile.' Jim stepped around her and walked quickly to the hardware store and harness shop. To his surprise the girl came in right behind him.

'Mr. Steel, I do believe that we need you with our party. Two guides are better than one. I'll

25

pay you four hundred dollars to take us in, if we bring Becky back.'

'Dead or alive?'

Sarah West Edwards gasped. Her eyes widened and she caught the beginning of a sob. Then slowly she nodded.

'Forget it, Mrs. Edwards. Any man going in there is asking to get his head cut off. Those are savages in there who hate all whites. And they've got good reason. They would rather kill you and me than find out what we wanted. How would you like to see me hung upside down and stripped, and watch while a half dozen Chiricahua squaws start skinning me alive? They make a game of it, seeing who can get the biggest section of white skin all in one piece before the victim dies. Is that what you want to see?'

Her face twisted in horror as he talked, and she shrank back. Now she stepped toward him. 'You're trying to frighten me, aren't you?'

'Damn right. Rather scare you than dig your grave.'

'Sir, don't swear in front of my sister!'

The voice came from behind Jim. He turned slowly, but it was only the foppish tenderfoot from the saloon.

'Is this thing really your brother?' Jim asked Sarah. She nodded. 'Then keep him on a leash in your hotel room until the eastbound stage comes through or somebody's likely to shoot him just for the hell of it. We don't see many

26

like him out here.'

'Then you flatly refuse to help us?'

'Every way I can, ma'am.'

'Well I never!'

'Got some business needs tending to down near Tombstone. Anybody would be crazy to try to take two horses into them mountains, much less four or five. Ask the sheriff.'

'I . . . I already have.'

'Lady, you want to commit suicide, you go right ahead. But me, I'm not ready to die with you.'

She stepped back and talked quietly with her brother as Jim began selecting the supplies he wanted. He had planned to travel light and eat off the land, but there wasn't that much game along here. He'd have to stop at the general store and get some beans and flour and a few cans of things. Maybe some dried fruit and jerky, too.

He waited until the girl and her brother left the store before he added a small hatchet and a short-handled pick to his stack. The thought of Becky West came up as he stood there. If her owner were good to her she might be alive, but it would be worse than stupid to go see. To try to get her out of Cochise's stronghold would be a real fool's plan.

When he settled his bill, the idea pushed to the surface again. Jim snorted and shook his head as he took his flour sack of goods outside and walked toward the stable.

Jim brushed down Hamlet, his big buckskin, and added an extra feeding of oats. He and Hamlet had been together for three years now, ever since Jim found him being sold outside a saloon. Hamlet had been part of a traveling dramatic show troupe. On his last performance he tried to steal the show and then nipped the woman star right on her behind. The star demanded that the horse go, so Hamlet was promptly auctioned. Hamlet was the stage name and it seemed to stick.

Jim patted the big animal and turned, picking up his saddlebags and the sack of hardware. He was headed for the general store.

'That's a good looking buckskin,' Sarah West Edwards said. She stood directly in his path halfway into the stable.

'This is no place for you to be,' he said curtly.

'I've been in stables all my life. I'm army, remember?' She smiled. 'Mr. Steel, we still need your help, desperately. My brother and I don't know this country or the Indians. You do. We're determined to go in there and find Becky.' She took a step forward deeper into the gloom of the deserted stable.

'Mr. Steel, I'd be very grateful if you would help us. Just *ever so grateful*.' She stood close to him, holding her shoulders back, and he saw she had taken off the little jacket she wore. Her breasts lifted and pushed tightly against the soft white blouse. Her eyes caught his, her lips parted.

28

As Jim watched her, surprise was his first reaction. He'd seen the offer done better in dozens of trail saloons and fancy lady parlors in a dozen states. But she was class, society, a general's daughter from the East. He knew he could seal the bargain with one touch, one kiss, and then he could do anything he wanted right there in the stable or in his hotel room. But he knew it would never work, because there wasn't the slightest chance of his keeping his half of that kind of a bargain.

'Mrs. Edwards,' he said gently. 'I won't take a woman into those mountains, because I wouldn't go into the stronghold myself. You're too beautiful to die so young. I'm going south tomorrow. If I see anything or hear about your sister, I'll get word to you here at the hotel.'

The woman stepped away, hurt showing deeply on her face, reflecting not only her failure to convince him about rescuing Becky, but physical rejection too.

'That won't help me much, will it, Mr. Steel? That isn't what I need.'

'I know exactly what you need. A husband to keep you in line and safe at home where you belong.'

Her smile faded, and anger replaced it. 'You're just what he said you are, Mr. Steel. You're half crook and half gentleman, but you think only of yourself.'

She put both hands on her hips and glared at him, her small chin thrust forward, her eyes sparking fire.

'Just don't get lost, Jim Steel. I have the feeling we'll be seeing each other again.' The girl turned and marched out of the livery stable toward the hotel. She was furious but she didn't try to stop the enticing wiggle of her hips as she moved.

Jim grinned as he watched her out of sight, then he put his saddlebags down and scratched his beard. That was one damn pretty woman, even when she was mad. He wouldn't mind seeing her again, but the chances were slim now. He wondered how she had learned so much about him so quickly? Somebody in Tucson was a blabbermouth. He'd have to cover his tracks well when he left in the morning, and follow the Tombstone trail for ten miles at least before he cut east.

Jim decided on the soft bed and the bath. He'd get an early start in the morning. The story of Swift Hawk still burned in his mind, and his memory brought back the details of the map to the wall of gold. The more he thought about the old Indian and his death, the more Jim knew that the map was genuine. A dying Chiricahua simply did not lie on his death bed. The Life-giver would not permit it. Jim wondered how many days it would take him to get to the lost valley.

He realized he needed a shave. Seeing a beautiful woman made him think about his appearance. He'd stock up his saddlebags, then check in at the hotel and have that long, hot bath.

An hour later, as he settled into the hot water of the tub, he tried to forget the tiny, delightful woman with the good figure and the hat with long plumes. But he couldn't.

CHAPTER THREE

Jim Steel bellied into the hot brown dust at the crest of the steep arroyo and edged forward so he could look past a ragged branch of mesquite. His eyes, perpetually squinted from years under the blazing sun, narrowed even more now as he stared down the burning desert wash ahead. All he could see were clumps of stunted sage, a few spires of dead cactus, and one spindly greasewood wand stabbing up from the sand and gray brown rocks.

Where the hell was that Chiricahua?

The Indian was out there somewhere in the half-mile of desert oven, along with the rattlesnakes, mice, and ground squirrels. Jim had worked against the Chiricahua long enough to know they were the cleverest and most crafty of all the Indians in tracking, desert camouflage, and silent, invisible movement. Now he was locked in a one-against-one battle with this brave. An hour ago Jim realized that only one of them could come out of the contest

31

alive. That's when he took the offensive.

For three hours he had played the game of hound and hare with the unknown red man, not sure which role was his. Jim had spotted the Indian first as the brave moved through the parched desert at a trot, his bow and arrows clutched in his left hand. He was a hunter, ranging far during the dry season to find game for his wickiup. He had passed close enough to Jim's daytime hiding blind so he saw the Indian's ribs and the determined look on his face. It meant there was some hunger in the Chiricahua camp.

Before the Indian had run a quarter of a mile, Jim's horse nickered as he caught the new scent. The brave heard the alien sound—and the silent battle was on.

This was Chiricahua land and no one, not even the army, penetrated into the Dragoon mountains of southern Arizona Territory. Especially not in July, 1867. The whole Apache nation was continually at war with the white-eyes, but the Chiricahuas had retreated deep into the rugged Dragoon Mountains and lived off the land. They left the white man alone, so the army did not try to rout them from their stronghold.

As soon as the Chiricahua heard the horse he vanished. Jim had mounted at once and ridden hard, punishing his big buckskin, angry because he had not had time to get to the animal to hold his muzzle shut and prevent him from making the noise. After an hour's hard ride, Jim left the horse in a draw under a chimney rock and backtracked, watching for his quarry.

The United States Cavalry learned quickly that the crafty Chiricahua could travel as fast through the Arizona and New Mexico sun-baked deserts and mountains on foot as a company of soldiers could on horses. Evidently the brave had done just that, and when Jim doubled back the red man spotted the maneuver and launched an offensive.

Jim had escaped the first death-charge only because of the glint of sunlight off a polished blade. Now he had turned the advantage around and was waiting for the brave to come to him.

Jim lay motionless in the blistering sun even though a small rock prodded him in the chest. He remained there for half an hour, moving only his eyes, sweeping them back and forth across the scene below in a practiced gesture he had learned and refined during two years when he wore a blue uniform in the Great War. Sweat dripped off his nose. His shirt long ago had plastered wetly to his back. But his patience would pay off. He would outwait the brave. He had learned his stalking and outdoor lore from experts. When he was growing up in the wilds of Montana his only playmates had been young Crow Indian boys.

Two hundred yards below, Jim saw a brown

shadow sliding slowly from one large brown rock toward another. It was the Chiricahua, his movement so slow it would have been missed by anyone not searching for exactly that form of locomotion. Jim blinked, relaxing the tension, then watched the blob again. The brown shadow never became a man. Not an arm or a leg showed, yet the brave seemed to flow from one point to another. The movements were irregular, spaced out, but carefully controlled.

Jim lined out the brave's course of travel and spotted a ravine that merged with the main water course below. Another hundred feet and the red man would reach the concealment of the sandy bank of the wash.

He waited until the brown form vanished behind a large rock, then he wormed silently down through the hot sand and stones away from the crest. He rolled over, wiping sweat from his face, and slithered farther down the ravine. Then he stood and ran up the arroyo. He held the six-gun against his right thigh, forgetting for a moment the special tie-down strap he had made so he could snap the gun tightly in the holster when it wasn't needed. A Case fighting knife with an eight-inch blade flapped on his left hip, but over his chest hung the weapon he would have to use against the brave—a stout Indian bow he had bought at the general store in Tucson. It had a new string made of tough, twisted animal gut that would last for years. He also had a dozen twenty-eight-inch arrows that were straight and Indian feathered. The arrow was a silent, deadly weapon, and the only kind he could use on his secret trip through Apache land.

He had worked with the bow and practiced until he could hit what he aimed at. He proved it by killing rabbits during the first three days of his trip. A rifle or pistol shot in this range would bring immediate attention from a wandering Indian scout or hunter. That would lead to a larger party and a fast and silent death, Chiricahua style.

Jim ran hard for the point where the ravine met the higher ridgeline. Sweat drained down his sides under his blue denim shirt. He edged to the very top of the arroyo and scanned the sun-blistered wash below.

The brown smudge was gone. Farther to his right he saw the bent-over form of the Indian. He had coated his body with sand and dust, and now he ran up the very start of the second gully. Soon he stood and trotted at a steady pace which Jim knew he could maintain for twelve hours up and down the hills and through the desert even at 110 degrees.

Jim eased back below the ridgeline. He took off the bow and strung it, then nocked one of his arrows. The point was a medium sized Indian arrowhead about two inches long and tied to the shaft. What he needed now was a four-inch heavy war arrowhead and heavy shaft. Now he had to kill a man.

Jim teased as he watched the Indian running toward him. He had no illusions about his skill with the bow against the Chiricahua. The Indian was more proficient at killing with his bow, and this brave had only that in mind— killing Jim so he could claim the horse and supplies to help feed his camp. So Jim had to count on surprise for a quick and killing attack.

The Indian paused, scanned the ridgelines around him, tested the string in his own short bow, then ran again, angling directly toward Jim's position only a hundred feet away.

Jim waited, then came up on one knee and sighted on the dusty brown chest. When the Indian straightened to check the ridge again, Jim let the arrow go. He was surprised at how straight and true it flew. It hit the Indian in the left breast, too high to kill, but spun him backward. The brave clutched his bow as he fell.

Jim nocked another arrow but before he could shoot it a blazing pain surged in his left upper arm. The brave had fired back at him already!

Jim grabbed his arm. A three-inch, sharp-tipped obsidian arrowhead had slashed into his arm an inch from the outer side. It glanced off the bone and drove straight on through, cutting denim and flesh as if it were soft cheese. The spent, bloody arrow lay just behind him.

36

Blood ran from the wound.

Jim looked down at the red man. He was staring up the slope, feebly trying to get another arrow into his bow. His right hand wouldn't work for him. Jim let go of his own arm, felt the burning, searing pain. He tightened his jaw and put his second arrow on the string.

Jim could almost smell the dank wetness of a rain-drenched wood, see the four men on his advance party back in '63. They had been told to scout out the enemy without making contact and bring back an estimate of the forces just across the river. But they had a fire fight and one boy of sixteen in gray had been captured. That was when Jim learned that a reconnoitering patrol couldn't take prisoners. It was war. They were over two miles from their own lines. The boy had to die. So did this Chiricahua.

He pulled back the bow string and shot. The arrow caught the Indian in the chest and rolled him down the slope. The brave didn't move for five minutes. Jim held his shoulder to slow the bleeding as he watched the hunter below. At last he knew it was up to him.

Jim drew his big knife and stepped over the edge of the ridge, unmindful now of the blood that ran down his arm, that dripped off his fingers and into the dry sand. He went down the ravine carefully, his knife ready in his right hand. He'd seen too many 'dead' Indians spring up and kill.

The brave's eyes were closed. Jim nudged him with a foot. Before Jim could make a sound the Chiricahua grabbed his boot and twisted it, pitching Jim to the ground. The hot sun sparkled off the blade as the Indian's knife moved.

Jim had time only to lunge forward, plunging his knife into the red belly, angling it upward under the ribcage. The Indian's knife fell from his fingers as the double-edged blade sliced deeply into his heart.

A long sigh spilled from Jim's lungs as he stared at the dead man. He didn't like killing Indians, especially on their home ground. His arm throbbed. He looked it over critically now, cut a section off the tail of his shirt with the bloody knife and, with the help of his teeth and right hand, tied a make-do bandage around his arm to stop the bleeding.

He flexed his arm and winced. It would take a month or two to heal properly. He didn't have a month. He didn't have a week. The tribe would miss this brave in two days. Jim tried to raise his left hand over his head and groaned.

Tough, he told himself. Just too damn bad. He'd have to make the best of it. He wasn't going to quit now.

First he had to get rid of the body. For half an hour he scooped sand out of the side of the ravine with his right hand. He used the Indian's knife to dig out hard spots until he had a hole nearly deep enough to hide the man. He rolled him into the depression and pushed sand and rocks over him. On top of the long pile he put twenty-pound rocks. That would have to do. It should work until the first good rain.

With luck no prowling coyote would happen by this way for a day or two. After that it would be a matter of hours until the sharp nosed coyote sniffed out the remains and unearthed them. Then the buzzards would move in, pinpointing the body for the alerted Chiricahua. Three days, he needed at least three days.

*   *   *

A half-hour later Jim found his horse, Hamlet, and scanned the peaks of the Dragoon Mountains in front of him. He couldn't see Diablo Mountain yet. It had to be more to the east and south of him. He had been moving that direction for three nights now, and decided he was still two days ride from the stronghold. He looked up at the sun and saw there were six hours of daylight. Jim had to find another hiding spot until darkness. He checked over the little gully where he had left the horse under the chimney rock and decided it would work. He was far enough away from the desert floor and seemingly not on any kind of regularly used trail.

Again he went through the daytime blind

ritual, cutting a few of the dead greasewood and sage bushes to form a dense screen in front of the horse. It took him a half-hour to finish the job, then he swept out his tracks in front of the blind with a length of brush and stretched out in a smattering of shade with his head against a rock.

But sleep would not come. It was too damn hot to try to sleep. He kept hearing a father's plea and tried to forget it.

*   *   *

'For God's sakes, man, she's just a girl, eighteen. You know how those Chiricahua treat prisoners. She's only been gone for a week. If you get in there fast under a flag of truce, I know Cochise will listen to you.' The silver star twinkled on the army blue.

Sleep came at last and Jim dreamed. He saw a promontory, and an old Indian man almost naked, his wrinkled face turned to the heavens, singing his life-song, a placating petition, the song of a life almost over.

Then the dream changed and Jim thought he was awake. He looked down a narrow valley and saw a wall of gold, with the setting sun coming through a notch in the mountains, flashing brilliantly on a wall of pure gold, wider than five braves with outstretched hands.

Jim turned over in his sleep and woke up, his mind still filled with the old Indian's story

40

about the wall of gold. It had to be there, he'd heard too much about it over the years for it to be a myth. And with luck he would find it. For an hour he thought only of the gold before he slept again.

CHAPTER FOUR

It was just past six that evening when Jim gave up trying to sleep. He sharpened his knife, honing it carefully as only a man can do when he has plenty of time. He used the small double-sided oil stone until the eight-inch Case hunting knife shaved hairs off his arm. He polished it, checking the white and brown stag horn handle for cracks. The blade was his all-around knife, for cutting up a freshly killed deer, or for fighting. Three inches of the tip held a double edge like the old Bowie knives.

Jim couldn't travel yet. The sun still cast long shadows over the roughness of the Dragoon Mountain foothills, and his dust trail would show up for ten miles through the clear desert mountain air. Instead he cleaned the rifle he carried in his saddle boot, even though he was sure he wouldn't have to use it. By this time he had penetrated into the real Chiricahua country where any pistol or rifle shot would bring immediate attention. Whoever fired the shot would be hunted down and killed for his food, water, and horse. The firearms were only for Jim's final line of defense, if all other means failed.

He had no intention of using them. He would travel carefully, using his head, moving only after dark and holing up during daylight. Unless he stumbled into a hunting party at night, he should be able to walk right past Chief Cochise's wickiup without his ever knowing it. Jim was betting his life that he could.

He had a new rifle, a Yellow Boy, a seven-pound model 1866 Winchester 44.40. It was the best weapon he'd ever had. He got the twenty-six-inch barrel for more range, and this one had a lever action and held nine shots.

His pistol was the same, a Centennial New Model Army Revolver first made in 1860 in .44 caliber. He'd had the gun reworked by a gunsmith so it would take solid case ammunition, no more slow ball-and-cap loading for him. The revolver used the same 44.40 ammunition as his rifle, and he had two boxes of a hundred rounds each in his saddlebags.

Jim eyed the setting sun, pushed the .44 into his holster, and cleaned up camp. He had eaten a hot meal, using the driest twigs of cactus and dead mesquite he could find to produce a hot flame and absolutely no smoke. For five minutes he'd burned the fire to warm up his beans and boil coffee, then he put it out with sand, completely killing any smoke.

One plume of smoke in this country would attract the Indians' attention as much as a company of cavalry. Jim had laid out the odds and decided that he was smart enough and knew enough about the Chiricahua to slip through their homeland and not stir them up. Without the map from Swift Hawk he never would have tried it, but now a chance at the Apache wall of gold was too much to pass up.

He watched the shadows lengthen, scooped another six inches of sand over the fire pile just to make sure, and moved around his blind picking up every scrap of evidence that he had been there. As dusk settled, he used a dead mesquite branch to brush out his bootprints from the dust, then mounted Hamlet and carried the branch for a hundred yards before he dropped it.

Jim could still see a quarter of a mile. His head began turning as if it were on swivels, his eyes constantly moving, scanning the trail, working each side and ahead as far as he could see. In the daylight he had picked out his route eastward, angling for the jagged split in the ridgeline ahead. For about a mile he could continue straight east, then he'd have to make a small detour north around a finger ridge before he got back on his eastward course. Beyond the notch he was not sure exactly which way he would go. By then he would be high enough to see Diablo Mountain again, and that would determine his route.

He made good time, walking the beast, careful not to make any more noise than necessary. Once he heard a coyote howl and he stopped, listening to the tone of the bark. Then he heard a dozen more blend in, and he knew it was the real thing, a pack of coyotes serenading each other. There was no moon. He moved carefully. Once over a soft spot, he broke off a mesquite branch and dragged it in back of Hamlet on his rope, wiping out even the hoofprints of the horse. When he came to firmer footing, he carried the brush for a quarter of a mile before discarding it.

Twice he stopped and listened, his senses sharpened by the cool night air. He knew the slightest sound would travel for miles in the clean darkness. But nothing broke the gentle sighing of the soft breeze except the occasional night hawk's cry, and the scurry of small desert mice which came out in the safety of the night's blackness to search for food.

Jim watched the Big Dipper drop in the sky until it reached the point which told him the night was half over, then he pulled the buckskin to a stop. He was below the notch in the rim now, but the ridgeline looked too dangerous to attack blind. He would go as far as he could tonight, then wait until daylight to pick a safe route which he would use with the next darkness. It would slow him down, but that was the safe way, and better than to be

44

quickly dead. He wished now for a moon to light his path to the top, but it wasn't to be. Jim moved another quarter of a mile, selected a sharp-sided ravine with a smattering of mesquite and found enough dry chaparral nearby to use for a blind.

Jim dismounted and settled down to work. It had to look like a jumble of brush that had been carried downstream by a sudden torrent from a desert cloudburst. He jammed dead, tough mesquite brush into the sandy wash bottom, then put rocks and sand around them to help them stand. He piled up more of the dry chaparral torn loose in the rains, until he had a four-foot-high wall. He checked it from the front, made some changes and then broke down one side so it leaned in. On the way back from his frontal inspection he wiped out his footprints with a length of brush.

Utilizing the steep bank of the wash and the mesquite, he could shield himself and his mount from the three sides where there was the most chance of being spotted. The buckskin's light yellowish dun color blended well with the surrounding desert shades, and Jim decided he had made one of his best blinds. He was safe unless a wandering hunter decided to flush out this particular wash for rabbits.

Jim had finished before the Big Dipper touched the two o'clock point in its circle around the North Star, so he stretched out on his folded blanket and relaxed for a change in the coolness of the desert night air. It would be blistering hot again tomorrow, probably around a hundred degrees, much too hot to get any sleep. He looked in each direction around his small camp, but he saw no movement and heard no sound except one owl which hooted in welcome a quarter of a mile downstream. Gradually Jim let himself unwind. His hand slid over the butt of his .44 and his eyelids scraped closed. If anything larger than a mouse moved within a hundred feet of him, Jim would hear it and be awake. It was a kind of survival sleep he learned during the war, when he soon discovered a soundly sleeping soldier often turned out by morning to be a dead one.

Hamlet breathed deeply and stamped his feet, but Jim ignored it, and drifted off into his half sleep.

When he woke, the first streaks of dawn daggered into the blackness over the eastern peaks and ridges of the Dragoon Mountains. He opened his eyes without moving anything else, checked what he could see, then lifted his head and gradually looked around the blind, searching in increasing circle sweeps across the high dry hills. Nothing moved, not a horned toad, not a kangaroo mouse or sidewinder rattlesnake. It would be a long day. Much too warm for productive sleep, too dangerous to hunt for rabbits. He took the bow from beside the Yellow Boy rifle and wiped it off, then strung it and selected an arrow from his pack.

46

It was a willow reed, not entirely straight, and the tip made of chipped obsidian notched and tied around the split end of the shaft. This was not the most well-made arrow in the Territory, but it was deadly if it hit anything. He moved to the very front of the blind and sat, watching for a ground squirrel or rabbit. With luck one would come close enough so he could shoot it with an arrow and he'd have some fresh meat.

Jim estimated that two hours passed as he sat unmoving in the blind. Nothing had come close enough for a shot. He relaxed and reached for his canteen and saw a small lizard leap from a rock in alarm and scurry behind another rock. It had been less than two feet from Jim and so camouflaged by coloration that Jim hadn't seen it, and apparently it hadn't spotted him.

While he drank he checked in his memory the location of the next spring which Swift Hawk had pinpointed for him. Then he let his eyes sweep across the two miles of open valley in front of him. His gaze went past the distant figures the first time, but he stopped and looked again. There could be no mistake. About a mile away he saw two horses working his way, both with riders. Jim caught up his binoculars, a souvenir of the big war, and focused on the pair.

They weren't Indians, he was positive of that, but they were still too far away to tell much more. The one in front appeared smaller and, to his surprise, seemed to be following his trail. Jim gave a small moan of fury and sat down to wait. It had to mean trouble, he just wasn't sure what kind.

He had the Winchester ready and the six-gun in his hand, but he had the feeling he wouldn't be using them. As the pair came closer he confirmed his worst guess by looking through the army field glasses again.

'Sarah West Edwards and her brother,' Jim said out loud. Now how in the hell had they found his trail and tracked him? He shook his head and watched as they continued to dog his tracks to within fifty yards of the blind where he had brushed them out.

The girl on the lead horse looked at the brush marks which the wind hadn't erased yet, then studied the pile of mesquite. She urged her mount forward at a trot and slid off just outside the blind.

'Hello, Jim Steel. I figured you'd be moving faster.'

Jim stood, looking around the blind and waved them on in.

'Get in here before you warn the whole Apache nation that we're here ready to be roasted alive.' He let his temper simmer as they brought their mounts up the ravine and behind his partial shelter.

'What the hell are you doing traveling during the day?'

'I can't read sign at night, can you?' The girl

48

asked.

'You never should be out here anyway.'

'We knew we'd catch you, then we'd be safe.'

'Ha!' He scowled at her as he studied this small woman. She had on faded jeans, a wide-brimmed felt hat with a low crown, and a light jacket over a blouse. At least the colors were blue, brown, and gray.

'Girl, you have any idea what kind of chances you took coming in here this far by daylight?'

'No. When my baby sister is involved I don't stop and count up the chances. I figure whatever they are, Becky is important enough to take the risk.' She slid her hat off and shook out her hair letting it cascade in a red-flecked brown river down her shoulders. 'Mr. Steel, we didn't expect this to be easy.'

'Easy!' Jim paced over to Hamlet, working the anger out of himself. He stomped back. 'Not easy, impossible! Getting three people and three horses through the Chiricahua home country is not easy, it's absolutely impossible. Just as soon as it gets dark the three of us are turning around and getting out of here as fast as this horseflesh will take us.'

'No.'

Jim glared at her 'Lady, you're going if I have to tie you hand and foot and put you belly-down across your saddle!'

'Sir!' the man behind her said.

'Shutup!' Jim exploded. He turned toward

49

the foppish young man behind her. The tenderfoot's face had turned bright red from sunburn, his eyes watered, and he kept sniffling as if something irritated his nose.

'What kind of a man are you, letting your sister come in here? You crazy, or just stupid and weak?' Jim didn't expect an answer, and got only a screwed up face that evidently passed for anger and derision by the dude.

The girl had turned and walked to her horse, and she came back with a sack of food. 'About time for something to eat around here. You do eat, don't you, Mr. Steel?'

He ignored the question. 'How have you managed to get this far without a fight?'

A touch of a smile colored her pretty face. 'We did just what you did, even stayed in your blinds, only we used them at night. I learned tracking in Texas one summer when I was fourteen. An old Indian scout helped me, trained me for two months. I enjoyed it and he said I became quite proficient. That's not the sort of thing you forget.'

'No Indians spotted you?'

She had dropped to her knees in the sand, opened the sack.

'No. I thought it over, decided you had exaggerated the dangers, that you were probably off on a gold hunting excursion since you're called the gold man. I saw what you bought in the hardware store, then I checked to see if you bought any food at the general store

50

and found out what it was. Then I knew you were on a long ride, not just to Tombstone.'

'But the Chiricahua...'

'I knew you were bluffing after we were out for two days and nobody bothered us. Oh, we worked the land for what little concealment it offered. We stayed in washes and shadows when possible, moved and stopped, walked most of the time, and rode at dusk and dawn. But when we saw you tangle with that brave, I admit I was scared. When you didn't just shoot him with your rifle, I knew what you said must be true. You couldn't risk a rifle shot which would bring other braves. After that we were more careful, and I remembered a lot of tricks my old scout taught me. We didn't use a fire after that, either.'

Jim squatted across from her, flipping a small flat rock into the air and catching it.

'You're damn lucky, you know that? You two happened to be in the right places at just the right time, and you missed every Chiricahua. We'll be more careful going out.'

'But we can't go out, Mr. Steel. I thought I made that clear. We must find Becky. You've got to talk to Cochise.' Her hair moved, now perfectly framing her face; her bright eyes were seriously brown and concerned, her cheeks touched with a hint of suntan, her mouth partly open, showing white, even teeth.

'Mrs. Edwards, Cochise couldn't help you, even if we happened to be lucky enough to live

51

long enough to get to talk to him. This isn't like the officers' club at the Fort. There are no rules here. Not our rules, anyway. Your sister was captured by one man on a raid. She became his legal and rightful property by Apache law. He can do with her what he wishes. Cochise wouldn't take her away from him to give back to us. He wouldn't even consider it important enough to talk about.' Jim watched her, trying to see if he could scare her, make her angry, anything. He saw her small chin come up.

'Mrs. Edwards, didn't your Indian scout friend tell you about the Chiricahua and how they treat prisoners?'

'He was Sioux, he didn't know.'

'I don't know how else to tell you, Mrs. Edwards. It is best to believe that Becky is dead. If she isn't now, she will be before we reach her. All of our experiences with the Chiricahua tell us this. These are savages we're talking about, who have been cheated, lied to, massacred, driven off the lands they have called home for hundreds of years. Their tribes have been broken up, their trust violated a hundred thousand times. *They hate all whites.* There is no possible way we could even talk with them. You can't talk with an Indian who is trying with all his might to kill you.' He stood and still watched her. 'Now why don't you go ahead and eat, then get some rest. We'll be leaving here on our way back to Tucson just as soon as it gets dark.'

When she looked up, he saw defeat starting to edge into the tone of her voice. 'Can we have a fire?'

'I'll make it, we can burn it for ten minutes to boil coffee and make whatever you need it for.' He began gathering sticks for the fire, dead chaparral and dry, whitened cactus stalks. She watched everything he did and he was sure she could make an identical fire if he asked her.

She made coffee, then she mixed flour and water to a prepared dough she took from a jar and fried pan biscuits. She offered him two, and he discovered they were good.

Sarah Edwards suddenly put down the small frying pan. 'Oh, my goodness, you haven't officially met Harry. This is my brother, Harry West,' she said. 'Harry, this is Jim Steel the gold man.'

Just like they were in Boston or Atlanta in some fine parlor, Jim thought. He nodded at the strange young man. His riding outfit was unusual, a pair of blue silk pants and a red velvet shirt with long billowing sleeves. On his head he wore a soft cap with a small bill which gave him almost no sun protection. The tops of both his ears were white with sun blisters.

So far he had said almost nothing. Now he gave a slight bow, then turned and went over to his mount. Jim watched as Harry refreshed himself from a silver flask. Great, just great, Jim thought. It was bad enough that he was a greenhorn, but now he was drinking on the trail. Jim made a mental note to watch Harry West carefully.

When the meal was over, Sarah cleaned the utensils and packed them away in a bag tied to the back of her saddle.

Jim had returned to the front of the blind to watch the desert slopes for movement. Earlier he thought he had seen a dust trail, but he decided it could have been dust devils, those small whirlwinds which spin dust and dirt into the air, then fade away. But now, through the binoculars, he saw there was a horse and rider, perhaps two miles away, working across the very end of the valley north of them. A lone Apache hunter. He showed the Indian to Sarah.

'Mrs. Edwards, there are three hundred braves in the stronghold with their families. The Chiricahuas intend to stay there so they send out hunting parties on up to three days rides so the game in the immediate area won't be all killed off. They crisscross these hills and valleys all the time. There's some proof for you that we've got to get out of here just as soon as we can after it gets dark.'

Jim looked at the notch to the east regretfully. Long ago he had picked out his route up the steep slopes. Now he wouldn't be climbing that trail for at least a week.

'Mr. Steel, Becky is my sister, we've got to get her out.'

'Mrs. Edwards, have you ever seen your

54

father write letters to the wives of men killed in battle?'

'Yes.'

'It wasn't easy for him, was it? And the more details the survivors wanted, the harder it was. Becky is dead. Don't ask about the details; it will only be harder on you and your family.'

'Becky is a beautiful young girl, wouldn't one of the braves keep her as a wife ... a ... a mistress?'

'No, they might use her, pass her around for a while, but the squaws wouldn't allow anything permanent. The Apache squaws can be more vicious and savage than the men.' Jim watched her take a deep breath, saw her chin quiver. 'Now, Mrs. Edwards, I didn't mean to upset you. You better get some rest now. We're going to ride hard going out of here.'

'But Mr. Steel ... *she's my sister!*'

Jim knelt down in the sand beside her. 'Yes. That's a strong feeling. But we're not in Philadelphia or New Orleans or even St. Louis. We're in the middle of the uncivilized, dangerous frontier where life is cheap and death is sudden. Women are a wonderful and scarce commodity out here. I've been in towns where men outnumber the women fifty to one. I've been in mining camps where there were no women at all for two years. The men used to ride thirty miles to a small town and line up on a bench outside the saloon just to watch the two women in town walk to the general store.

55

Women in these parts of the West are treasured, protected, and spoiled beyond all measure. That's partly why I can't let you stay here. Besides, you're too pretty a girl to let the Apaches get.'

She saw he was sincere and dipped her head slightly in thanks.

'Mr. Steel, I recognize all that, and I thank you, but I'm not talking about generalities or women on the whole. Becky ... my little sister ... Becky is the one. I want her back!' Sarah dabbed at her eyes a moment. 'If we all can't go in, couldn't you go alone, slip in and scout them out, get close enough to see if she's even there, find out if she's still alive?' Her pleading eyes burned hard into Jim's and he shifted uncomfortably.

'Ma'am, you want me to sneak up on a camp full of Chiricahuas?'

'Yes, you could do it. You're good enough, as good at it as they are. I've been tracking you for three days, remember. I know a lot about you by the trail you leave.'

He wanted to say it was absolutely impossible. So why didn't he? The girl smiled again and he was more aware than ever what a beautiful, desirable woman she was. She sensed his indecision.

'We could find somewhere to hide for two or three days while you went to the stronghold. My father said Cochise felt so secure there he doesn't even have the usual sentries out. You

56

could get up close, watch camp for a while, learn if she's there and alive...'

The unfairness of it hit him. She was taking advantage of him because she was a woman, soft and beautiful. If a man tried something that unfair Jim would have knocked him down. But as he looked at her beautiful face, the sweep of her slender neck and the upthrust breasts, he was more aware than ever how she stirred him.

'Look, Mrs. Edwards, it's dangerous just *waiting* in this country. What if that brave we saw a few minutes ago decided he'd seen some rabbits run up this little ravine?'

'Mr. Steel, I'm taking the risk too, and I say it's worth it. If we can help Becky, any risk is reasonable!'

He was beaten then. There was a spot they could stay, an old cave he had used once before the Chiricahua moved into the stronghold, when he had been prospecting. It should be less than half a day's ride from the notch in the ridge above.

'Please, Mr. Steel, it means so much to me!'

'Look, I don't go for this "mister" stuff, call me Jim.'

'Well, thank you, I'd like that. You call me Sarah.'

Jim sighed. A pretty face usually didn't cloud his judgment. But this time it probably had. Damnit. But, as near as he could tell, the map to the wall of gold would take him well beyond the stronghold. So if he could leave these two at the cave and make a gentle probe, a quiet scouting mission toward the stronghold, it should be enough to satisfy her without any great danger.

'I'll probably regret it as long as I live—which might not be too long—but we'll try it. You can stay at a cave which is about half a day's ride ahead.'

'Oh, Jim! Thank you.' Tears battled with her eyelids and slipped down soft cheeks.

Jim had the impression she would have kissed him if Harry hadn't been watching. He stood. 'You better get that sleep, we'll be heading for the cave soon as it's dusk.'

'Yes, Jim. Yes, I will. And thank you so much!'

He watched her get a blanket from her saddle and lay it down in the half shade of the mesquite.

Harry sat to one side cleaning his fingernails.

'Honestly, this is just the filthiest country. I can't wait to get away from it.'

'I won't cry a bit when you go,' Jim said. The foppish young man closed his eyes and turned away from him. A short time later Jim had stretched out on his blanket in the partial shade. He was sweating already. It wouldn't be noon for two hours yet. He had settled down on his side so he could see half of the dry valley in front of him, guessing that he wouldn't be sleeping much. Women. Damn, they sure did

58

complicate a simple little trip, he thought.

Sarah looked a lot different in her trail clothes than she had three days ago in Tucson, but she was still the prettiest woman he'd ever seen. Her tongue and her wit were just as sharp as when she scolded him in town. Even now he hardly knew how she had talked him into this fools' gold try.

Sarah's scream brought Jim up to a squat, his gun hand automatically pulling his .44 from leather. Jim saw the girl on her knees ten feet from him staring at a rock. At the same instant he saw the pale-colored coiled snake and heard the tail rattle.

'Don't move!' he said softly. 'Just freeze right there!'

'I'll get him!' Harry West called loudly and Jim saw him holding a revolver in both hands, aiming at the snake.

'Don't shoot you fool!' Jim yelled at him. But even as he said it he remembered the Indian hunter in front of them, and Jim was on his feet running toward both his problems.

CHAPTER FIVE

Before he took a full step, Jim had holstered his gun and pulled out his big knife. His warning yell stopped Harry, who looked at Jim curiously. Then he saw the blade. Jim threw the

Case in one smooth movement as he ran. The cutting edge slashed into the coiled sidewinder, preventing it from striking. A moment later, both of Jim's heavy boots smashed down on the two-foot-long snake, crushing it. Jim made sure the sidewinder was dead before he retrieved his knife and wiped the blood from it onto his pants, then he kicked the dead carcass away from the horses into the wash.

Sarah still sat on her feet staring at the spot where the snake had been. 'Now I remember,' she said calmly. 'Never move a rock where a rattlesnake may be hiding.'

'Yes, ma'am. Sidewinders are little but they pack a nasty bite.' Jim tried to ride herd on his temper, but he couldn't. 'Sarah, why did you do that? It shows me one thing: you two are not cut out for this country. When darkness comes we're heading back for Tucson. This is no place for bumbling tenderfeet. Both of you made mistakes—little ones, sure—but that's all it takes in this country to get us all killed. If Harry had pulled that trigger, right now we would be riding hell-bent for our lives. There's no way we would have made it. So get used to the idea; we're heading back.'

Sarah got up and walked toward him. 'Jim, yell at me, hit me a couple of times for being dumb, but don't take us back to Tucson. We have to go get Becky. Did you forget so fast?'

'When my hide is at stake, lady, I can change my plans in a rush.' He scanned the sloping dry

60

wash and valley in front of it.

'Down,' he whispered. 'Both of you get down and don't move. We may have company!'

Jim crawled to the front of the blind, picked up his bow and arrows, and put the big knife within easy reaching distance. He lay flat to peer under the tangle of mesquite.

It didn't take a flash of sunlight off an arrowhead, or a trail of dust. Jim saw three braves dog trotting easily across the sun-baked desert. They were not more than three hundred yards away, so close Jim thought he could hear them breathing. Each brave carried game over his back: the first a coyote, the second a string of rabbits, and the third several small game birds. Their bows and three favorite arrows were held in their right hands as they ran mechanically across the desert on the shortest route back to the stronghold with their prizes.

Jim held his breath. He had no doubt he could silence all three with his rifle, but that would be foolish. With the bow he might be able to surprise them and nail one, and perhaps get the second with his knife, before he went down at the hand of the third brave.

He heard a clink of metal on metal behind him, and cursed silently. A horse stamped and started to make one of those impatient little throat noises, then stopped—and Jim let out his breath.

The three Chiricahuas ran a dozen steps

apart, and now Jim watched the last one fading off to the right, working his way up a large wash that must lead to the notch in the ridgeline above. The pass would be a natural funnel for the Indians hunting in this area, which meant he would have to be especially careful and alert when he used it.

He watched the three braves until they were out of sight and more than a mile away. When Jim turned he saw unconcealed fear changing Harry's face into a childish mask. Sarah lay near where she had been, her face forward, eyes on him now as he spoke. 'They missed us, and I don't know why. They could have seen half of that black horse of yours if they'd glanced up this way. Maybe some of our luck is going to be good.' He sat up and scratched his jaw where three day's growth of black beard had started to itch.

'The three Indians, they changed your plans again, didn't they?' Sarah said.

'Yep. Seems now it's just as dangerous to go back to town as to stay here. Must be a bunch of hunters out yet, and we're in the middle of them. I'll trade half a day of moving on to that cave instead of two and a half days hotfooting it out of here. Any objections?'

'Oh, no, Jim. That's good news.'

'I'd rather get back to Tucson,' Harry said. 'At least they have bathtubs there.'

Jim saw that the man had controlled his terror by now. He needed a good tongue

62

lashing, but Jim gave it up as a waste of breath before he started. The kid would simply have to be dragged along and watched so he stayed out of trouble.

'You two better settle back down and get that sleep. We've got a tough six-hour ride ahead of us going up the ridge, and I don't want either of you going to sleep in the saddle. I'll stand guard and wake you up half an hour before dusk. Now don't just lay there, get some shut-eye.'

'Yes, sir!' Sarah said, recognizing the snap of military authority he let creep into his command. She saluted, grinned, and folded her blanket in quarters before she lay down on it, facing away from Jim.

'You too, Harry.'

The man in the red velvet shirt made a childish face at Jim, then adjusted his blanket and lay down.

Jim went back to the front of the blind and scanned the desert again. Nothing moved.

He settled into a sitting position and tried to figure the odds. They should have no problems getting to the cave in the darkness. He'd recognize the last three or four miles. Once up the ridge and through the gap they should be safe, unless they ran into a hunting party pressing for home and travelling at night. But the odds were with them.

Three hours later, Jim woke Harry and told him to stand guard. 'Just watch the desert. If you see anything move—anything—come wake me up.'

Harry grumbled, but nodded, his childish anger gone.

'Remember, don't shoot that gun whatever you do!'

Jim tried to rest. He found he could do little but check on Harry every two or three minutes. At last he turned so he faced the girl, and away from her brother. Maybe that would help. At last he dozed, but he awoke with a feeling of danger and looked at Harry. The kid had slumped over with his head almost on his knees, and he was snoring with a roaring growl. Jim jumped up and slapped the youth awake.

'Stupid! You idiot! You trying to get us all killed? This ain't a church picnic.'

Harry rolled to one side to escape the punishment. Now he stood and brushed off his blue silk pants and velvet shirt. His childish, sassy face returned but he didn't speak. Instead he shrugged and took his blanket back toward the rear of the enclosure.

Jim worried now about his plan to go ahead. The kid was absolutely unreliable. Sarah would stand a better watch than Harry. They would soon be deeper inside hostile territory. Could he risk it with Harry? An idiot like Harry could get them all killed without even trying, especially without trying. He weighed that against the large numbers of hunters the

Chiricahuas had sent out. Wouldn't that mean more hunters in the area right around the stronghold as well?

Jim fumed and sweated as he checked the blistering desert valley in front of him. Then he refused to think about it any more. Maybe his plan to go forward was simply another way to get closer to the hidden valley, closer to the gold. He pushed it all out of his mind. Too much thinking clouded the problem, made the decisions too difficult.

Jim checked the sky. Two hours until sunset, then another hour before they could be moving. He rolled his blanket and tied it on behind his saddle, then packed everything he had taken from his saddlebag. He wanted to be ready to ride the instant they could. He admitted to himself that he wished he could simply pull out and leave them, let them worry about themselves. If it had been only the man, he would have done so in a flash. But, as he did with any woman in the West, he felt an unreasonable responsibility and protectiveness for Sarah.

*   *   *

Three hours later they were moving. Jim had re-established his route up the ridge, which turned out to be more rugged than he had guessed, but nothing a good quarter horse couldn't handle. He took the lead, with Harry next and Sarah as rear guard.

'Everyone has to be able to see everyone else all the time,' he told them just before they left. Sarah had been brushing out their foot and hoofprints inside the shelter. 'If you can't see the other two you're going too fast or too slow,' Jim said. Sarah caught the implications of putting Harry between them but, if her brother did, he didn't show it. His pout was gone but a new look of bored indifference clouded his face.

The route he had chosen wasn't a trail, just a series of rideable cutbacks that helped them zigzag their way to the top. Each pitch got steeper, and several times they stopped to listen and watch. Jim heard nothing unusual. Once he heard some large animal moving, and guessed it was a mountain lion.

'Let's stop. I'm getting tired,' Harry said. Jim ignored the plea and kept going until he heard a sharp call behind him. It was Sarah. He looked, but neither of the others was in sight. Jim found them twenty yards back. Harry sat on the ground taking a drink from his canteen.

'What the hell are you doing?' Jim snapped.

'For heaven's sakes, you can't just ignore a person like that. I told you I was tired.'

Jim brushed back both sides of his heavy black mustache and adjusted his .44 on his right hip so the kid could see him.

'Harry, you get back on that horse and ride with us and keep up, or I'm going to break both

66

your arms and tie you over your saddle. You savvy?'

'But ...' He turned to Sarah.

'He's right, Harry. You're acting like a school boy.'

'But ...'

'Move, now!' There was a sharp snap of command in Jim's voice that he seldom used. It remained Harry of his father's tone, and he stood, put the canteen away, and mounted his horse. Jim watched him, glad that at least the kid could ride.

They made good time after that. The notch turned out to be an earth slide of gigantic proportions, and it saved them over three hundred feet of climb. Once through the opening Jim moved to one side of what now showed as a faint trail. He couldn't see Diablo Mountain in the dark, so Jim began searching ten-year-old memories of the area. Snatches of remembered landmarks and the mental map from Swift Hawk came back and got them started along the right ridge. It was away from the faint trail he guessed the Apaches used on their hunting forays.

They rode the razor back ridgeline for half a mile, then moved into a scattering of brush and stunted trees. Jim scanned the valley on both sides of the ridge, and at last turned down the slope.

He heard no more complaints from the rear and saw that Harry was keeping up. Swift

67

Hawk's map turned out to be sketchy through this section, and Jim rode slowly, feeling his way, trying to establish landmarks, doubling back twice when he found he was on the wrong route. Harry grumbled each time, but Sarah only smiled encouragement.

After a three-hour struggle through dry ridges and blind valleys, Jim found the dry falls, and he was back on his mental map. The route was easier after that, and a half hour later Jim rode Hamlet into a cave with a partially blocked mouth.

It was huge, over a hundred and fifty feet long and twenty feet high. Numerous side branches afforded places for more security, and they chose one side cave fifty feet from the mouth, far enough so the smoke from a fire would dissipate partially inside the cave before it could escape.

'Oh, it's big!' Sarah said, dismounting and looking around. 'I bet prehistoric men used this cave to live in. Look at the smoke stains on the walls.'

Jim had never considered cavemen living here, but now it did sound sensible. He had seen by the Big Dipper outside that it was nearly four A.M. They had been riding for almost eight hours. As soon as they ground tied their mounts, Jim went outside to find firewood, and returned with an armload of dry twigs from dead chaparral and cactus. The abundance of firewood near the cave entrance told Jim that the Chiricahuas had not been using this cave as a stop-over point on hunts. Did that mean the stronghold was within five or six hours ride? He wondered.

Dust in the entrance of the cave showed him that nothing but coyotes and rabbits had been in the cave for many months. He relaxed just a little. The cave should be a safe haven for a few days at least.

As he built a small cooking fire, Sarah brought out the evening's food. Coffee, beans, and hardtack.

'Too late to move on tonight,' Jim said. 'I'll get some real sleep and be ready with the next darkness.'

'Thank you, Jim. I really do appreciate this, and my prayers will be with you for a safe journey.'

'I'll need that at least, and all the luck I can scrape up.'

She opened the can of beans, then got another one and heated them over the fire. The coffee smelled good and Jim poured out half a cup before it had boiled long enough to be done.

'Tired?' he asked her.

'Yes, but excited too, and anxious. Becky just has to be all right.' She looked up at him, her face serious. 'Yes, I know what you've told me, but I'm going to hold out hope for as long as I can.'

After the meal, Jim cleaned up the utensils,

69

sand washing them and laying them out on a
stone. Sarah went to her blanket and lay down,
and Jim saw that she was sleeping soundly a
few minutes later.

Jim went to the horses, glad for the moist
coolness of the cave. He wanted to unsaddle
them all, but he decided it was too dangerous
this deep into hostile country. Maybe when he
left tomorrow he could take the saddles off the
other two. Jim rubbed down Hamlet,
loosening the cinches on all the saddles, and
just as he finished, Harry walked up.

'That's a fine looking buckskin,' Harry said.

Jim had a slight frown on his face. It was the
first half-normal thing he'd heard the boy say.
He thought of him as a boy even though he was
older than Sarah, which made him twenty-two
or three. Jim kept rubbing down Hamlet.

'Look, no hard feelings. I said I was sorry
about what happened back there. I'm not
much of an outdoorsman.' He paused and
looked at Jim carefully. 'You have a good
strong body, Jim, do you know that? Fine legs,
chest.' As he talked, Harry took off his red
velvet shirt. 'At least it's not hot in here.'

Jim rubbed down Hamlet more, curious
what the kid was building to. He moved to the
other side of Hamlet so he wasn't looking at
Harry.

'You mind if I take off my pants?'

'I don't care if you strip naked. But getting
some sleep would be smarter.'

70

When Jim looked back the man's pants were off and his drawers were coming down. 'I'd like to get some sleep, with you, Jim. Oh, I could take care of you, make you very happy, Jim. Let me try. Please let me try with you just once. I'll be much better for you than Sarah.'

Jim's mouth fell open in astonishment as the real meaning of what the foppish dude was saying came through to him. Jim darted under Hamlet's neck and took two quick strides toward the naked man. This kid was strange all right, just like the men he had seen in San Francisco who made love to men. A damn roomie, a homosexual!

He slammed into Harry chest-high and battered him to the ground. Then Jim's knees landed on Harry's chest, pinning him in the dirt. Jim's razor sharp knife blade pressed against Harry's pale throat and Harry began whimpering, begging for his life.

CHAPTER SIX

Cochise, the great *nan-tan* of the Chiricahuas who had led his people into the safety of the stronghold, sat cross-legged at the front of his wickiup looking on in silence as two ten-year-old boys practiced stalking each other in the grasses near the small stream. It was good. His people were safe here, for a few winters at least.

71

It was his mighty stronghold where not even the pony soldiers dared to come, his high haven in the Dragoon mountains where the white-eyes had never been.

In this *rancheria* many of his followers were gathered, and more Chiricahuas joined him each moon. The place itself was not a fortress as some thought, but a large box-ended valley, with sharp cliffs on three sides. Big enough for his people to live and rest in peace. At two points cool springs flowed the year around and formed a small stream that wandered down the valley.

Cochise felt secure here, isolated from the *Meh-hi-kanos*, protected by many days ride through barren and rugged mountains to the nearest settlement of the white-eyes. Here for a while his people could put the white man's treachery behind them, and live as they had for hundreds of years before the invaders came. And he could forget the deceit at Apache pass, and how the pony soldiers had tricked his father-in-law, Mangas Colorado, and murdered him with no reason at old Fort McLean.

The great Indian chief brushed the spider webs of memory from his head and watched the squaws cutting venison into long thin strips to be hung in the sun and dried until they hardened and cured, so they would be good eating when the cold winds blew. There was much jerky to make, and the strips had to be tended and turned.

Game was being taken in far areas, safeguarding the supply near at hand. A chief had many small life-things to consider for the good of his people. He had heard that some squaws had planted corn down by the stream. Cochise did not look with favor on farming, reserving the usual Apache scorn for 'farmer Indians,' but he would gladly eat of the corn when it was harvested.

For two winters his Chiricahuas had stayed in this place, safe and contented, as in the old days. No fighting with the *Meh-hi-kanos*, no running from the brown-skinned *Naka-yes* below the Rio Grande. They must rest, grow strong, and gain more followers, for Cochise had many tall thoughts, and knew that their safety here would not last forever. One day the blue-coated pony soldiers would come and he and the braves must be ready.

Cochise watched the two boys on the marshy pond where the stream widened, and rested. There many ducks came to feed. For days the boys had floated hollow gourds into the midst of the flock. At first the ducks flew away, but when they saw the gourds day after day they accepted them. This day the boys had opened the gourds and cut eye holes in them, then they put them over their heads and, crouching low in the water with only the gourds showing, they waded and swam slowly downstream into the midst of the ducks. Quickly they jerked a dozen of the fat birds under the water and into weighted strings, then floated on past with a good catch for supper.

The braves went out hunting daily, taking any game they could find in the hills except bear. All the Chiricahuas had a truce with the bear, they were brothers with the bruin and would not harm him. Often the boys of the tribe did track the brown bears for practice, sometimes following the beasts to a honey tree. Honey was the only sweet the Chiricahuas had. It was a high point in any boy's life when he found a bee tree and struggled back to camp with a deerskin sack bulging with the tasty crushed honey comb he had stolen from the angry bees. Usually his eyes were swollen shut, his torso and legs covered with sting welts, and his belly half sick from gorging on the great delicacy on the way back to camp.

The honey was a favorite of all Indians and Cochise especially liked it with pinole, made from flour of the mesquite bean and acorn.

Again Cochise studied his stronghold. What else could he do to protect his people? He tried to think tall again, but could not. The stream caught his attention. It was the life-blood of the stronghold. Arrow canes grew beside the water, and even mulberry branches to use to make bows. He sighed. He was thinking of olden days, long past. Lances and arrows would not win battles against bullets of the pony soldiers. He could win small battles, with many Indians and few white-eyes but it was never so. The *Meh-hi-kanos* kept coming, like swarms of flying ants, never stopping. More and more of them came with each new moon.

Cochise looked up as he heard strange laughter from one side of the camp. Three braves watched something. Soon she came in sight, and he saw Golden Hair, the captive from a recent raid. She was white of skin and her yellow hair hung to her waist. He sighed as he watched her teasing the braves. She slowly took off the top part of her clothes until she was bare to the waist, her big breasts swinging free, bouncing and jiggling for the pleasure of the braves.

She was different. It was unusual for a squaw to act this way, and her boldness surprised the braves who were not pleased, but not able to take direct action either, since she was the slave woman of Lost Knife. He had taken her prisoner when he and two others attacked a stagecoach and brought back six strong horses. They also carried a box filled with thin round pieces of squaw's clay with pictures on it. But Lost Knife owned Golden Hair. He could do with her as he pleased.

Lost Knife had not been wise so far, Cochise knew, but it was still a private matter. He would see that it did not get out of control. But already Lost Knife had taken the squaw as his own and refused another brave's request to use her. A knife fight followed and both Indians had been badly cut.

Cochise had called Lost Knife and reminded him about the horse which two braves had claimed only two full hands of days ago. Each had equal claim to the animal and neither would back down. Cochise had taken his captured pistol and shot the horse twice in the head, killing it, and divided the meat up to the whole *rancheria*. Lost Knife understood. Everyone knew that a fine horse was worth many squaws. He knew he must control Golden Hair if he were to keep her. But Lost Knife was so delighted by this young white-eye woman he could deny her nothing, and certainly he would not tie her in his wickiup.

For five days he had controlled her, but now she was out again and causing trouble. Her bare-breasted flaunting would mean a problem, Cochise knew. He had hoped secretly that Lost Knife's squaw would do away with Yellow Hair before now. But his woman was heavy with a new child and had no hot blood left in her. Cochise rose and walked from his wickiup past the ceremonial fire area and toward the shade where Yellow Hair danced.

'Come on, big strong Indian, give me a try,' Yellow Hair said. 'Think you're man enough to make me beg you? You got another thing coming, you savage! I'm tougher than all of you. I can take all you got and yell for more. Come on, line up. Who wants to be first?' She lay down on the grass and pulled up her skirts.

76

One brave lunged at her, a second tripped him, and they rolled in the dirt. The third drew his knife and warned the other two away.

'Enough!' Cochise said softly. All three braves heard the command and relaxed.

'Well, the big one, Chief Cochise,' Golden Hair said in Spanish. 'Come to rescue your poor little Indian braves?'

Cochise signaled for a squaw to come. He told the Indian in his own language to keep Golden Hair in a wickiup, even if she had to tie her up.

To Cochise it was a minor irritant. The she-cat was not worth troubling about. However, she could not be allowed to cause a loss of any braves, or upset the camp. He might need his warriors at any time. It simply did not occur to him that anyone would be interested in finding the captive, or that they would be bold enough to come looking for her. She was only a woman, a young one with no skills, a slave, a spoil of war, and she had no value to anyone other than her owner.

He was still thinking of the squaw's clay that was on the coach of many horses. The *Me-hi-kanos* treasured it highly, and called it *oro*, gold. Would the pony soldiers come with many rifles and big guns to find the chest of round squaw's clay? If he saw them coming he would take the chest and leave it near a signal fire directly in their path. They would find it, and leave. He folded his arms, frowning. All

77

troubles could be solved by tall thinking.

Yes, that was a good plan. Lost Knife had told his *nan-tan* that the guards had fought to protect the *oro* until all were killed. It must be very important. Cochise nodded as he walked back to his wickiup. No longer did the worry of the *oro* hang around his neck as a large stone when he swam in deep water.

An hour later Cochise had inspected the herd of ponies enclosed next to the wall of the cliff. They were in a safe place and were being fed better than Apache ponies usually were. Cochise insisted on this, knowing the value they would have in a hard fight with the pony soldiers. As he walked back toward his wickiup, he saw Golden Hair near the ceremonial fire circle. Now she had taken off her skirts and stood naked, dancing and screeching at two braves who fought before her with clubs.

Cochise ran twenty steps and called out, 'Stop.' The fighters rolled on the grass exhausted.

A dozen squaws hurried up and braves moved toward the scene. As Cochise got there the squaw he had ordered to hold Golden Hair limped into the circle. She had a bruise on her head and blood streaked her old face.

'There will be no more fighting for the body of Golden Hair,' Cochise said. By this time Lost Knife had struggled from his wickiup, his right arm wrapped with healing leaves and a

78

poultice of dry bark and berries. He shouted at Golden Hair, pushing her to the ground, then he moved in front of Cochise. But the great *nan-tan* stopped him with a wave of his hand.

'Lost Knife, you have not controlled your property. Your spoils of the raid are forfeited. Bind her hands and feet and lay Golden Hair on the living rock. Soon I will decide what will be done with her.'

He did not speak in Spanish, so the white girl did not know what he said. She sat silently where she had been pushed to the ground. She had stirred them up, that was certain. But she knew she could trade her body to the chief for a pony and a guide out of here. It was what she had been trying to do since the day she arrived.

'Chief, big *jefe*, when can we talk? I have many pleasures for you that your own squaws would never think of. It will be very good.' She stood and stretched, displaying her fine body to him.

Cochise stared at her as if she were fully clothed. 'For you and me, Golden Hair, the talking is over, it is done,' he said in Spanish.

She shivered as he said it. What in the world did he mean by that? She tried to dart away, suddenly frightened. But two squaws caught her and roughly tied her hands and feet with strips of rawhide. They carried her to a flat, polished stone in the ceremonial fire circle and laid her on it. Then the squaws began dancing around her, each one jabbing her, slapping her, pinching her white flesh or pulling at her long blonde hair.

She tried to dodge them, and saw the delight build in their eyes. For a moment she recalled tales of how Indian women were twice as cruel as the braves, especially against white women. She winced at the pain and saw pleasure in their faces.

Now, for the first time since the Indian had ripped off her blouse back at the stagecoach, Becky West was frightened.

CHAPTER SEVEN

Jim had felt an overpowering disgust when he saw the 'fancy men' in San Francisco, but there he had simply walked away from them. Here he couldn't. He stared down at one of the same breed, and naked to boot. Jim pressed his big knife hard against Harry West's throat, his surging anger building toward a peak. He should slash the blade forward and rid the world of this filth! Instead he drew the knife delicately across the tightly stretched neck flesh, barely slicing open the skin.

Harry West choked out a sob and fainted.

Jim stood and kicked the silent figure in the side. He wanted to go right on kicking, but he remembered the girl, and walked back to the small fire and his cooling cup of coffee. When he looked at Sarah he saw she was still sleeping, faced away from the scene. She couldn't have seen much of it anyway, in the thin light that filtered over there from the fire.

Jim looked down and saw he still held the knife. He checked the blade and flicked off a spot of blood, then tried to put it back in its sheath. His hand was shaking. Jim didn't mind facing a gunman or an Apache with only his knife, but that little scene near the horses had unnerved him. He at last fit the knife in its scabbard and began feeding small twigs into the fire. The smoke collected in the high ceiling and would not be noticed even if it did escape outside later. He looked back toward the horses but couldn't see if Harry had come around. If he didn't soon, Jim would splash some water in his face. The pansy had to be dressed before Sarah woke up.

Jim kicked at a rock in a sudden anger. How in hell did he get into these messy situations? He should have turned the pair around the moment he saw them and sent them back to town. Jim drank from the cup of cold coffee and threw the rest out.

Maybe he should ride out now, get as close as he could to the stronghold and hole up? That way he wouldn't have to be near that damn homosexual. Jim squatted by the fire and caught a tight rein on his surging emotions. That wasn't being smart. He had planned what to do, to wait for next darkness, and that's

81

what he would do. He could scout around outside tomorrow, maybe find a rabbit to shoot with his bow. He could stay away from the dude and he wouldn't tell Sarah anything about it. He stood, satisfied with his decision, and walked toward the horses until he saw that Harry was gone from where he had fallen. Jim was glad; now he could roll out his blanket and get some sleep.

And he did sleep. Twice he woke before he could see light coming in through the entrance to the cave. The first time the horses got restless, smelling water but not sure where it came from. The second time a dark shape came toward him and Jim knew it must be Harry. Jim cocked his six-gun and the resounding click stopped the dark figure.

'Get some sleep, Harry,' Jim said. 'I've decided I'm not going to kill you after all.' The shadow faded away and Jim heard muffled sobbing. He uncocked the six-gun and put it down by his right hand and went back to sleep, knowing he had read the young fag correctly. The kids's big try for revenge had been made, he didn't have guts enough to try again.

Sometime near daybreak, Jim heard Sarah get up and start getting food ready. After that he couldn't sleep. He went over and over his chances of getting through the narrow entrance to the stronghold, and knew they were not good. The pathway in was barely wide enough for a horse to walk. One good rifleman with enough ammunition could hold off a whole division of soldiers at that point. And there was no other way in, not past those sharp bluffs, unless you had a rope a thousand feet long.

Nor could he ride to the cliff faces above the stronghold and see enough through his binoculars. It was much too great a distance for him to pick out a white girl if she were there.

Jim got up. He had not even unlaced his boots. On the trail he always slept ready for immediate action.

'You're up early,' Sarah said. 'I thought you would sleep until noon.'

Jim started to say that he couldn't sleep when there was a pretty girl around to look at and talk to, but he stopped himself. 'I thought you might want some fresh water. There's a small spring in one of these caves, according to Swift Hawk.'

'Jim, before you get water, we need to have a talk.' She looked up at him, her eyes serious. 'Harry's still sleeping.' She looked away. 'Jim, you know he's not quite the same as other men.'

'A real tenderfoot, a dude.'

'Well, yes, he's not right for this country. He's a little different in other ways, too.' She glanced up at Jim, then quickly away. 'I guess I'm asking you to go easy on him. He's going to make mistakes, get into trouble. But he's the only brother I've got. Please, don't be too harsh with him.'

Jim looked down at her and realized just how beautiful she was. He understood what she said. She must already know about her brother's peculiar habits. 'Sure, Sarah, I'll try to go easy. But if he starts to do something that's gonna get us all killed, I'll get mean as hell.'

'That's fine Jim. You know we're leaning on you, out here, and I appreciate it.'

Jim touched his hat and went to find the spring. It seeped from a mossy green rock and flowed a dozen yards to where some Indian had scooped out a basin, a yard across and half that deep. Jim tasted the water first, decided it was pure, and leaned down and drank. Then he filled two quart containers and the three canteens. When he carried them back, Sarah was fixing breakfast.

'Oatmeal mush!' Jim said when he came up to the fire. 'My old mother used to fix that.'

Sarah smiled up at him, her eyes happy now. 'But I bet you never had it with beef jerky for breakfast.'

He ate. It was good. The coffee was hot and the jerky did taste good despite the hour. He noticed that Harry had already eaten and retreated to his own private area. Jim didn't talk during the meal, and Sarah watched him curiously.

'Are you worried about going in there tonight?'

84

'Yes, I live longer when I worry.'

'Will it be extremely difficult?'

'Yes. I haven't been near that valley for eight years. It's changed. Cochise probably has scouts out, guards at various places. I should know where they are.'

'But Father said Cochise had relaxed his guards,' Sarah said, pushing the brown hair back off her face. The corner of her eyes wrinkled as she talked.

Jim shook his head. 'Not Cochise. He's a war chief, a fighter. He'll never really relax anywhere until he goes to the big sleep.'

'Big sleep, is that what the Apaches call death?'

'Right. Is there any more of that oatmeal?'

After the meal Jim worked the area around the cave mouth, first checking it for any sign of humans, then bringing in mole wood, larger pieces so they could keep a fire going all night. On the last trip outside he said he'd be gone for a while, and took the bow, five arrows and his knife. His first shot was at a squirrel which he missed. Jim retrieved the arrow and almost at once had a twenty-foot shot at a rabbit. The arrow caught it just behind the front legs, killing it instantly.

On the rest of his scouting mission, Jim moved cautiously from scrub oak to an occasional pine that he found growing in this higher elevation where the mountains drew more rainfall. He remained as motionless as possible when he was beside a tree, but he could spot no movement, no indication that any Indians or any big game were present. He felt there must be some deer around and probably a few elk that had wandered down from higher elevations, but he saw no sign.

All during his hunting trip he was trying to remember the approaches to the stronghold. Back in 1859 he had been on a prospecting trip into the fringes of the Dragoon Mountains looking for gold. That was before the Chiricahuas had retreated here.

He chanced on a pair of Indian hunters, who had ranged far from their wickiups, had found their last two waterholes dry, and now were out of the precious liquid. Jim gave them half his supply and led them to a spring he knew of half a day's ride away. They spoke in Spanish and Jim found out one of the men was Cochise, then a subchief in the band. He told Jim about a beautiful valley of waters and said Jim should see it.

Cochise and the other man led Jim into the valley back there eight years ago. It was now called the stronghold, but all Jim could remember were high canyons with smooth rock walls. There had been dozens of blind arroyos, black oak and madrona mixed in with the mesquite and cactus, and more and more of the tall, stately pine trees. He remembered they had climbed several thousand feet to get to the place. The narrow trail winding between sheer cliffs was etched in his memory, but he wasn't sure yet how to get there.

Jim left the comforting shade of a scrub oak and ran across an open place to reach the shadow of a canyon wall on the other side. It was time to move back toward the cave. He walked slowly and with care along the dry water course. A hundred yards ahead he saw three rabbits feeding on some new grass shoots. Jim moved up slowly, cautiously. At fifty feet he drew an arrow, sighted in, and shot, and had a second arrow nocked before the first hit. The first missed, but his second arrow stopped one of the three rabbits. Jim claimed it, retrieving both arrows and putting them back in the quiver over his back.

He cleaned the two animals and moved toward the cave. Despite his eagerness to get inside the shelter, he watched the entrance for six minutes before he left his hiding place and entered quickly. As soon as he stepped inside he faded to one side and remained motionless. In the dim light he saw and heard only the two persons he had left there. He walked silently up behind Sarah, who was making fresh coffee.

'How about rabbit stew for supper?'

'Oooooooooooohhhhhhh!' Sarah shrieked. Then she saw it was Jim. 'You frightened me! How did you sneak up so quietly?'

'Easy. You weren't watching. If I had been a Chiricahua, you would have been nothing but a pretty scalp on my belt by now. You've got to watch that cave door. Before I leave we'll set up some sort of a warning device there.'

'Did you say rabbit stew?'

He held out the two rabbits. 'Get your biggest pot.' Jim skinned out one rabbit and cut it into pieces with his knife. Sarah had a pot of water starting to boil over the fire to cook it in. The second rabbit he left unskinned. He hung it in one of the small caves to keep it as cool as possible.

'Skin out the other one and cook it tomorrow. Can you do that, Sarah?'

'Yes, I think so. I watched you do this one.'

Jim left the fire and went to the spring where he had a long drink of water, then he moved the horses up and let them drink their fill. The spring died out a dozen feet beyond the pool, where it simply ran back into the soft soil of the cave floor and vanished underground. The water in the pool would be pure again in five minutes. When the horses were satisfied he picketed them inside the cave again and went back to his blanket. He saw there were two blankets there now.

Sarah put another small stick under the cooking rabbit. 'I thought you might like a little extra padding,' she said, motioning to the blankets.

'I've slept so long on hard ground . . .'

'But you would take a featherbed if I had one?'

'Sure would, thanks,' He dropped on the

pallet. 'Wake me up when the stew's done, if that's supper.' He paused. 'And if you sit on the other side of the fire, you'll be able to watch the entrance part of the time.'

She moved where he suggested. She had found some rocks and had made a passable fire ring, with a small cooking fire in the center. She had laid flat rocks at each side, where she could place a coffee can and edge the rabbit stew into the flames.

Jim had seen Harry sulking at the back of the cave, but he tried not to think about the half-man and concentrated on going to sleep. It was an art he had learned in the big war, when you had to grab sleep anytime you got a chance. Jim closed his eyes and in a minute and a half he was sleeping.

Two hours later, Sarah tasted the boiled rabbit and added a little more salt. She wished she had some vegetables to put in it for a real rabbit stew, but this would have to do. She wondered what time of day it was, but she had left her pendant watch back in her hotel room, fearing she might lose it. Sarah walked to the cave mouth and tried to see the sun, but she couldn't. Oh, dear, did that mean it was too late for Jim to be starting? She went toward his blanket, stopped, then went forward. Sarah knew he was worried about going to look for Becky. Perhaps she shouldn't have tried to talk him into it. After all, he was the one taking most of the risk. And what would she and

Harry do if he left and didn't come back at all? She reached for his shoulder.

'I'm awake,' Jim said, and lowered the six-gun which had come up suddenly, aimed at her heart. 'Don't sneak up on me that way, please. Sometimes I react quickly when I wake up.'

She watched him put the gun away. 'Oh, dear! I certainly won't do that again. I'll call from across the room ... the cave.' She waved toward the fire. 'Your rabbit supper is done. We have some pan-fried biscuits and rabbit and coffee, of course. Hungry?'

'No strawberry preserves or pumpkin pie?'

'Well, I ...' she laughed then, sensing the tease.

The meal was satisfying, and filling. Harry came up to eat, grudgingly, but he wouldn't look at Jim and spoke only to Sarah. The three of them licked the rabbit bones clean, and Sarah said she'd cook the second one the next day.

Jim had decided to travel as lightly as he could. He left the Yellow Boy rifle, and all the food except some jerky, three of the pan fried biscuits, and a sack filled with dried fruit. He tied two canteens to his saddle and rode to the cave entrance. Jim studied it from the outside when he rode Hamlet out, then decided to cut some brush and cover the lower half of the opening. Anyone coming in would have to move the brush first.

Sarah watched him from inside, her face

serious. 'Thank you, Jim. I'll sleep easier now.' She frowned and blinked. 'You ... you be careful.' Sarah stopped. 'Jim, you don't really have to go at all. It's too dangerous, isn't it? Just a silly woman's idea. I had no right to ask you to take such a risk. I'm sorry. Jim, you don't have to go at all.'

Jim had been watching her closely and he saw her bite her lower lip after she said it. He pulled Hamlet's head around and mounted. 'But I do have to go. I said I would. I'll find out what I can.' He grinned trying to break up the serious tone. 'Relax now, Sarah. I'm not about to get myself killed in there. I'd never forgive myself.' He waved and walked the big buckskin down the arroyo and out of sight of the cave.

*   *   *

Jim had moved slowly all through the new darkness. As he rode along he found the faint trail he had left at the notch and followed it where he could. He remembered some of the trail now, even when the faint mark he had been following vanished. It was nearly midnight when he came to an area where a fork in the path gave him a choice. One ravine led up one side of the mountain, the other went the other direction. He had to be correct on this one. By this time he and Hamlet had climbed at least two thousand feet upward through a now

91

partially brushy landscape. Chaparral of many kinds grew along with the stately black oaks that were showing their fresh new green spring leaves, which were late appearing at this altitude. Jim wasn't sure how high it was right there, but he knew some of the Dragoon Mountain peaks went to over six thousand feet and grew white mantles of winter snow.

He chose the left fork, and after a hundred yards he knew he had taken the right one. Jim remembered the sudden zigzag in the canyon where a turbulent winter stream and summer cloudburst gushers had not been able to pound through a big granite boulder the size of the general store, so the persistent water had gouged a path around it. Jim decided he was still five miles of hard riding from the spot where he guessed Cochise might have his first lookout. His security would depend on how safe the war chief felt his stronghold really was.

Jim rode up the arroyo side, rattling down rocks as he climbed it toward the lightning-struck pine on the ridgeline. After that he followed the ridge and dug a chunk of jerky from his pocket to chew on.

By two A.M., Big Dipper time, he was nearing the first danger point. Now the pines were thicker, and the black oaks carpeted some of the small valleys. The trees were still sparse on the hills, demonstrating the meager rainfall, but were growing larger and more numerous as he climbed.

Jim paused beside a three-feet-thick pine and eyed the area ahead. The gentle wash he had been climbing along lately had flattened, and ahead he saw it narrow and vanish against a solid wall of granite that slanted nearly straight up for two hundred feet.

Yes, this was the place. The wash would squeeze in again and plunge into a slice through the rock wall. He pulled Hamlet into a small screen of brush and tied him. In the thin moonlight he could not be sure he saw enough. He needed a closer look. He would leave the horse and move ahead scouting out the place on foot.

It was as he remembered. The solid rock wall opened narrowly, not large enough for a team of horses to drive through. Quietly, like an Indian, Jim moved along the sandy river bottom, until he was halfway through the canyon. He faded from shadow to shadow, moving when he could see another few feet ahead. He was nearly at the far end of the narrow slice when he heard a horse nicker. He wasn't sure if it came from in back or ahead of him. Jim moved quicker now, to rocks, then past a bare spot and out the other end of the rock tunnel to the side of a solitary pine. It was here he would find trouble if Cochise had anyone watching this place.

Jim remained motionless, his eyes and ears straining to pick up anything unusual. He saw them as he turned. Where before there had been only open grass, now two wickiups stood. This was the trail into the lower valley, the farthest limits of the stronghold. And now Cochise had relegated some braves to live here as an advance guard.

Jim froze against the tree. He could see no watcher, no sentry, which must mean that one was there. No fires burned in the wickiups, no smoke came from the hole in the center of the roof. Two horses stamped somewhere in back of the brush houses.

Jim slid slowly to the ground and lay perfectly still. He didn't move anything but his eyes for five minutes. Nothing showed. He waited ten minutes more before he heard a baby cry. The sound was quickly quieted. Jim studied the complex again and saw three more wickiups in back of the first two. He wondered if he should wait here for daylight, find a hiding spot, and check out this forward unit. If one of these braves had captured Becky West, this was where she would be, and not at the main *rancheria* in the big valley above. So he had to wait and look over the place, but he would have to ride Hamlet back a mile or more first and hide him well off the trail. Jim faded from one tree to another, moving back toward the entrance canyon. He was almost there when something bothered him, something felt wrong. Jim drew his big knife and moved cautiously. He was about to step into the mouth of the narrow slice in the rock, when a figure jumped into the space in front of him.

'Who are you?' the brave asked in Spanish.

Jim understood the question but didn't know how to answer.

'Iyeeeeeeeeeeee! You are a white-eye. No white-eye can move so well, so like a Chiricahua!'

'I come in peace,' Jim said in Spanish. 'I seek the white-eye squaw.'

The brave in front of him either didn't understand or decided the time for palavering was over. The Chiricahua drove straight ahead with his knife, aiming a killing blow at Jim's heart.

CHAPTER EIGHT

Jim's own knife swung upward, and the eight-inch blade met the Indian's smaller steel. The Case hand-guard brushed the knife aside harmlessly. Jim had crouched automatically in the Indian knife-fighting stance, holding the big blade in front of him as he would a sword, ready to slice either way or stab straight ahead. The reflex was natural because it had been battered into him when he had played with the Crow Indian boys near his home as he grew up. They had practiced knife fighting with wooden knives five hours every day the summer he was thirteen, awarding points for a cut, more for a kill.

The Chiricahua, if surprised by Jim's evident skill with a blade, did not show it. He began another attack, designed to put his opponent down quickly, without killing him at once, for *nan-tan* Cochise would want to talk with him. The slash, counter, fake, and sudden lunge forward produced no results for the brave. It had worked many times before. The Indian hesitated and took a small step backward.

It was the first hint of indecision that Jim had seen from the red man and he had been waiting for it. He drove in, anticipating the Indian's lurch to the side. Jim swung his foot forward sharply, his heavy boot connecting with the brave's shin, bringing a sudden howl of pain. Jim kept on the attack. He parried away the lighter knife thrust and countered quickly, slashing the brave's arm.

'I must see *nan-tan* Cochise at once,' Jim said loudly in Spanish.

The surging hatred of the Indian blocked out what the white-eye had said. He had been hurt, humiliated, and now he must kill this invader quickly. But his right arm hurt where the blade had kissed it with red blood. The Indian lunged again, forgetting the delicate, almost dancing movements that are so vital in good knife fighting. He had not held his anger in his heart for a dozen sunsets, and his sudden fury slowed him, telegraphed his movements.

Jim saw the brave wasn't listening. He

parried another thrust, faked a side slash, then dropped his arm and powered straight ahead with the big killing knife. The brave had no time to dart away. He was off balance, expecting an attack from the side, and his body came forward to meet the double-pointed blade. Jim felt it strike flesh, saw it slice cleanly between two ribs and drive six inches into the Indian's heart.

Broken Toe, a brave of twenty-five winters, kept moving toward him. The stag horn handle tore from Jim's hand, and a dead man fell on his back at Jim's feet. His eyes were open and glassy, his arm bleeding, but no red stain appeared yet on his bare chest.

Jim knew the man was dead. Now what? A dead sentry on post would alarm and alert the whole stronghold. Jim thought of putting the brave on a horse and taking him a dozen miles into the brush. But a missing sentry was just as bad. Cochise would be doubly watchful. Jim started to draw his big knife from the man's chest, then he paused. The blood would flow when the weapon was removed. First he had to think.

Slowly a plan grew. He searched for the brave's knife and found it. Then he picked up the Indian and carried him toward the wickiups. Jim put him down near a plot of bare ground. There he removed his own knife and plunged the Indian's into the wound. It bled very little. Now Jim used his thumb and hand in the dust on the open space and made a set of large cougar tracks across the ground. No Indian could miss them. It could lend some credence to the idea that the brave was fighting a cougar when he accidentally stabbed himself. To help prove the story, Jim took his knife and made four claw marks down the Indian's chest below the knife.

On his way back to the narrow gorge, Jim brushed out all traces of his bootprints. At the fight scene he scooped up the dried blood splatters, then he brushed out the marks with a cut branch and retreated through the dry wash to where he had left Hamlet. He mounted and rode a mile into the wild brush country before he tied the horse in a thick cluster of madrona and mesquite. Jim retraced his steps to the trail and checked it in the moonlight. Surprisingly, he found hoofprints of several horses which were shod, so his horseshoe marks would not cause alarm.

Running now, he made it through the narrow vertical slit in the rocks and pressed against his observation pine inside the valley. Nothing stirred in the Indian camp. It was nearing four A.M. He looked over the country and decided he should move away from the wickiups, to the side where the valley opened. Soon he found four young pines growing around an older tree. He used the young ones, climbing up them to gain the branches of the taller tree. Then, more than fifty feet off the ground, on the side of the tree away from the wickiups, he found three branches where he could sit. He cut a few lower branches and wove them into a kind of screen giving him good protection from eyes in the wickiups.

The sun was tingeing the eastern sky with probes of light before he was done. He unslung his binoculars and looked at the Wickiups.

They were the usual brush huts of the Apaches. Round in shape and domed on top, with a smoke hole in the center of the roof. The poles that formed the structure were jammed into the earth, then bent over on top and tied together with vines or strips of rawhide. Brush was woven into the holes, to form a thatch. Over the thatch went the tanned hides of deer, elk, even cougar, to make the house waterproof.

Only four had been completed, Jim saw now, with work still to be done on the fifth. Building a wickiup was a woman's task.

The squaws were up first in camp, taking live coals from inside to start outside cooking fires. They went about their work quietly until one squaw shouted when she found the dead brave. At once the camp rumbled with a flurry of action, with men, women, and children running from place to place. One brave took command and ordered everyone else from the death scene except three other braves. They looked at the body, then began checking the grounds for sign. Jim was afraid that many of the cougar tracks he had so carefully produced had been trampled out by bare feet. But the brave in command found at least one of the prints and called the others to look at it.

The track couldn't be mistaken, it was good. Jim had practiced making trails with the Crow boys. On the cougar he had always been the best.

As Jim watched, one of the braves ran to the pole corral behind the wickiups, caught a horse, pulled a hackamore over its head, and rode out of camp fast, moving up the valley. Jim knew he was headed for the main *rancheria* to report to Cochise.

Jim took the glasses and checked each face in the camp below. There was none with blonde hair and a white face. Becky West was not there. At least he knew that much. If the brave decided the dead man had not been accidentally killed by his own knife, there was a good chance Jim would not leave the small valley alive. He considered the possibility, wondering how long they would search. He had his .44 in his holster and twenty of the long 44.40 rounds in his belt. But that wouldn't hold off even four braves for long, once they knew where he was.

As the minutes dragged out into an hour, Jim began to feel he might have fooled them. It could be a small but vital victory. As the sun slanted into the pine, Jim realized he had left both canteens on Hamlet's saddle. He told

100

himself he wasn't thirsty, but he looked longingly at the stream which flowed less than a hundred yards away.

Now all he could do was watch and wait. He chewed on some jerky but found that it made him all the more thirsty. Before the sun had risen halfway to noon, ten horsemen came into the camp from up-valley. Jim scanned each face with the powerful glasses, but he didn't recognize any of them. And there was no white woman with them.

Now it seemed that a new brave took over, directing some of the men to search the area. Others went riding toward the slice-in-rock wall, evidently to check down the trail. But Jim could only sit and wait and wonder what they were deciding. At no time did any of the braves look into the area around his pine tree home. Jim would have given ten ounces of gold to know what the Chiricahuas were thinking.

Ne-oh-Pye, one of Cochise's subchiefs, stared at the dead brave, Broken Toe. He had ridden with him for years in many fine battles. One fact Ne-oh-Pye knew for certain, this brave had not taken his own life. The more he looked at the cougar tracks, the more he disbelieved them. How could an Indian swing at a big cat, miss, and hit himself in his own chest? No Indian worth his name was that clumsy with a knife. And the cougar claws on his chest didn't seem right. Unless they were starving, the mountain cats avoided Indians.

Ne-oh-Pye could not decide.

But if the brave was not fighting a cougar, it left only two other explanations. One, some renegade Indians from another tribe had invaded the stronghold, killed the brave, and fled, or a white-eye may have blundered in and done the same. If this were not the case, the other explanation was hard to believe. It meant that some person from the stronghold had killed Broken Toe and made it look like a cougar. He did not like the idea of having to suggest this to *nan-tan* Cochise. But it must be done.

Ne-oh-Pye sent two more men out to scout the surrounding hills just in back of the slice-in-rock. He signaled to the four braves who lived in the camp to mount their ponies, and Ne-oh-Pye rode with them as four of his braves followed. The men would talk with Chief Cochise and he would determine if any of them were guilty of the death of Broken Toe. It would be decided in three days.

High above in the pine tree, Jim couldn't believe it when the Indians rode away. He began to understand a little when he saw the four braves from camp get their ponies from the corral. Either they were suspects or they were going to make a report to Cochise.

The day dragged on. Jim wanted to sleep but couldn't. He had no way to tie himself into the tree. He saw some of the Indian scouts return, check in at the camp, and then ride on to the main *rancheria*. Still he waited.

Just before dusk he saw a guard posted. The Indian sat behind a small shrub fifty feet from the slice-in-rock, and this one had a rifle.

At long last darkness came, and Jim began his slow trip down the tree. He was so stiff he could hardly move. But he had to, and without making a sound. He climbed down slowly too, for fear the sharp-eyed guard might be looking his way. Jim decided that three of the braves from the *rancheria* had stayed at this camp.

Once on the ground, Jim moved up the valley like a scout on patrol, staying in the shadows of the shrubs and trees until he was a quarter of a mile from the guard, then he chanced a quiet, careful trip to the small stream. He ducked his head under, then came up and drank until he thought that he would pop. It had been a long time since he had wanted a drink of water that much.

When he wormed back into the brush, he moved north again, coming soon to the narrow, twisting trail that would lead him up around the mountain and into the fabled stronghold. Jim knew there was no place to hide once he began the steep climb up the narrow trail. Some of the trail had been blasted from the face of the cliff with stolen gunpowder. It never was more than four feet wide, and in places much less. One misstep could send him hundreds of feet to his death below. But there was no other way in. He reasoned that there would be no more movement between the two camps now that night had fallen.

Jim adjusted the six-gun on his hip and checked his knife, then began jogging up the narrow trail. The quicker he got over it and to the valley above, the less time he would be in naked danger.

Jim kept running. Only once did he stop, and then to edge delicately past a spot in the trail where a slide had carried away a three-foot section of the trail. He wondered how the horses did it. When he was on the far side he saw that the Indian ponies jumped the narrow slide.

When he came out at the top of the hard-rock trail, he paused in the shadow of an overhang and studied the serene valley. He could hear water, smell smoke. The fires of 300 braves would be hard to conceal anywhere. But where were their guards? One below must also mean another one here. He spent fifteen minutes sweeping the nearby locations where lookouts could be stationed. He had just about given up, when he saw a brave near a tree. Jim used his binoculars and watched the Chiricahua until he slid away from the tree in the opposite direction. Jim darted a dozen paces into the first patch of brush he could find inside the valley and not far from the sheer face of the cliff. He was ready to growl like a bear if the lookout had heard him. But after five more minutes Jim spotted the guard working up the far side of the valley.

Now Jim began his cautious approach to the *rancheria*. It was well after midnight before he moved far enough up the valley to see the first wickiup. As he came closer he saw that most of them were on the other side of the small stream and clustered around a larger one that must be for the chief. He spotted in the pale moonlight a ceremonial fire circle.

But the stream interested him more. He worked his way to it by crawling through bear grass, and found a small forest of arrow reeds, also called willows, and some thorny chaparral which grew near and in the water. There were other brush and marsh grasses around, and it seemed an ideal spot for concealment.

Jim worked forward until he was directly opposite the great ceremonial fire circle. The stream was a little over a hundred yards from the circle, with the brambles and willow thick along his side of the river. When dawn came he could slide into the water and use a hollow reed to breathe with, lowering his head into the water up to his eyes. No one would be looking for him, and even if they were it would be tough to spot him among the dense willows.

As he waited through the chill of the rest of the night, he wondered if Cochise did have three hundred warriors. That would mean three hundred wickiups, and there weren't that many here, maybe a hundred. But just the

105

thought of even a hundred skillful, bloodthirsty Chiricahua braves hunting for him made Jim shiver. That must not happen. He was here as an observer, not a rescue party. If he got any heroic ideas, he would remind himself of the hundred ways of killing a prisoner the Apaches bragged about.

Jim watched the Big Dipper work slowly around the North Star and at last, dawn crept in. As it did, Jim slid into the water. He gasped at the icy touch of it, remembering it came from higher melting snows. He adapted to it as well as he could, staying well back from the edge of the reeds, trying to protect himself from both sides of the creek. He found a stud branch to hang the binoculars and six-gun on, and tried not to think about being so cold. Shivers ran through him, his teeth chattered, and then he thought about the heat of the desert just two days before and he relaxed.

Jim watched the camp come to life. Squaws started fires, small hunting parties moved out, some on horses, some on foot. Soon the smell of cooking food came to him. He chewed on a piece of wet jerky from his pocket and tried to talk himself out of the numbness that crept into his hands and legs.

Once he dozed off for a moment and his head dropped forward into the water where he blew a dozen bubbles. He jerked up and after that concentrated on finding a hollow reed he could use for breathing if he needed to. He found one, cut it and tested it. It worked best when he held his nose underwater and then sucked in and blew out the air.

Jim heard some kind of commotion beyond the ceremonial circle, but he couldn't see what happened. Someone came from the chief's big wickiup. Jim guessed it was Cochise but he couldn't tell. He had forgotten what the chief looked like.

After that the camp quieted down. For two hours he saw common camp activities, boys playing war, women making jerky and tanning hides, some working on clay pots and others scraping deer skins. Jim watched each new face with the binoculars but saw no white-eye. When he put down the glasses he spotted two gourds floating down the stream. They were large and as they passed him and headed for the pool below where ducks had landed, he thought they had mask-like eye holes in them.

Jim used the glasses again and caught movement near the ceremonial fire circle. He thought he heard someone yelling. Was it his imagination or was that a woman's voice screeching in English? He listened again, and checked the area with the glasses. He saw only two braves with clubs in a mock battle. Then he lifted his brows. The braves were not in a pretend fight, they were serious about it.

He heard the shrieks again and a woman danced into view. She was naked and she was urging the braves on. Her skin was pale and

107

Jim looked quickly at her hair. With a low moan he realized who she was. Becky West was still alive and naked in the middle of the Chiricahua stronghold!

CHAPTER NINE

Jim watched the braves fighting. They seemed ready to kill each other, slashing, swinging the heavy clubs. Becky West ran around them, evidently encouraging each, laughing, yelping for joy.

Then a third figure jumped between the two fighters, and Jim, a hundred yards away, heard the shouted command to stop. The braves ceased swinging and glared at each other, ready to continue at the first excuse. Jim could not hear what the third man said, but soon Becky was seized by squaws and tied hand and foot and laid on the big flat stone in the ceremonial fire circle.

As soon as Jim saw them tie Becky, he knew she was in for trouble, but there still might be time to save her. If he could storm out of there and run up to Cochise and talk with him, remind him how he had saved him eight years ago in the desert by loaning him some water. The only trouble with that idea was he would never make it halfway to the fire circle. Some brave would get him with an arrow or a knife first. Then he would join Becky on the sacrificial rock for whatever Cochise had planned. He closed his eyes and tried to think it through. Nothing.

Even though his body was shaking from the chill water, he felt sweat bead his forehead. The chief had looked angry when Jim watched him through the glasses. Now he strode around the fire circle three times. Jim watched the squaws screeching and poking and pinching Becky. Some wound their hands in her waist-length blonde hair and made strange faces.

Chief Cochise returned and stood over the girl. Then he gave several quick commands and the squaws danced around the flat rock shouting wildly with delight. They began slapping Becky, pulling her hair, scratching her.

Jim felt a heavy dread creep into his heart. He had heard about situations like this with the Apaches. He shivered in the water, but the shiver was not from the cold, rather from fear for the girl's safety.

Braves ran up with three long poles which they tied together at the top and set up in a pyramid over the stone where Becky lay. They threw a rope over the crossed tops and let it dangle down. Then they caught Becky's kicking feet, and secured her ankles with the rope.

'Oh, my God, no!' Jim whispered in anguish. He knew about the Apache's hanging a victim head down. It was unspeakable. Silently he watched as her arms were tied to her sides. She began screaming as they hoisted her by her ankles until her head was three feet over the rock.

On a signal from Cochise the squaws surged in with their sharp knives and cut off Becky's long blonde hair, each squaw getting as much of it as she could. Several slashes on Becky's head glistened red with blood.

Jim sank lower in the water, a fear that he had never known tearing and ripping at his very soul. Jim could predict exactly what would happen to the girl now. He knew and he still couldn't believe it, couldn't accept it, not even when the fear came which was not for his own safety, but a fear for someone else, who had skidded into an unreturnable and terrible pathway to a horrible death.

The squaws ran back, each with pitch sticks and dry wood. The eldest of the group pushed the others away and took the honor of building the fire. She used one glowing coal, added shavings of pine-sap pitch, and then larger and larger sticks until she had a small fire six inches across. Above it Becky felt the heat and smoke and began coughing, then screaming.

Through the field glasses he saw blood running down her head, dripping from her quarter-inch stubble of hair. Her mouth came open again, and he heard her screams piercing through the laughter and derision of the squaws.

One squaw maintained the fire's size steadily. She kept adding as much fuel as would burn, and now the blaze was leaping a foot high over the rock. The screams from Becky stopped. She seemed to be talking now to Cochise, who stood nearby. She was pleading with him, arguing for her life. She gasped as the rope holding her slipped and she slid down six inches toward the fire. Becky screamed in raw terror.

Low in the cold river, with only his eyes and nose showing, Jim closed his eyes as he saw tufts of her hair blaze up and then die out. Becky screamed, with new cries of fright and horror piling on top of one another until they reached a continual horrendous expression of anguish.

On signal a brave lowered her another six inches until her head, now totally bare, hung only a foot above the dancing flames.

Becky's screams turned into hysterical blubberings, incoherent wailings, mixed with a few English and Spanish words. The squaws danced, flaunting their small coups of blonde hair as they went around and around the rock. They cheered each time the girl dropped lower toward the fire.

Jim sank his face into the water. He couldn't watch anymore, simply couldn't! He remembered vividly the three wagons he had found once years ago only hours after an

111

Apache raid. The goods, horses, women, and children had been all taken away, but the three men had been tied upside down on the wagon wheels and fires burned under their heads. Jim had never forgotten the unbelievably gruesome results.

Jim came up for air and he had to look. Becky's head had begun to blacken from the soot, her ears were black too, and soon her eyebrows would burn off. Her mouth moved as she tried to protest with a desperate will to survive.

Jim looked away and almost vomited. He washed off his face, and tried looking at the peaceful stream and the ducks below. He remembered his .44 six-gun. He could snatch it from the branch stub where he had hung it and come out shooting. He could get several of them, perhaps even cut her down! But after his gun was empty, he would be chopped to pieces or be hung alongside the girl, to stare down at his own last bonfire.

When Jim looked across the stream again, he saw two braves hoisting the girl upward to three feet over the flames. Had they relented? Were they going to spare her? Becky seemed to understand what happened, and she revived a little. She cried out to Cochise for his help. When the squaws heard her call they knew she was conscious again, and able to experience more pain. They took burning sticks from the fire they had prepared, and pressed them into

112

her soft flesh. They began at her neck, burning ugly welts into her skin, watching her twist and scream out in pain. New burn marks pocked her inner thighs, then they concentrated on her breasts, burning her thirty times, and with each scream from the white-eye, the squaws whooped out their joy and satisfaction. Before they stopped, her breasts were bloody, scorched masses of raw flesh. Only then did the eldest squaw signal for the victim to be lowered over the fire again.

This time Becky was dropped until her head was barely eight inches from the flames. The squaws quieted, sat around the rock and watched, waiting. Becky gave one last agonizing scream, then passed out. In the silence Jim could hear the crackling of the fire. He moved the glasses to Cochise's face, and saw it firm, unmoving, perhaps even slightly disinterested. He was performing a ritual duty, but he was thinking about something else.

Jim wished he could swim underwater down the stream, to escape the torture of watching the last few moments of Becky West's life. He fought against watching it, but some power turned his eyes back on the unfortunate girl. Her head blackened more, and her skin began to char. Jim knew she was dead or near death. The temperature inside her head must be too high for life. Soon her blood would begin to boil and she would be gone.

There was a murmur of delight from the

113

watching Indians as blood began to trickle from Becky's nose. Three or four minutes later blood burst from one ear and the squaws cheered. Now the fire was built higher, hotter, until the flames licked at her skull.

Jim fought the urge to try to leave, to crawl, swim, run, steal a horse, any way to get out of there! But he held his terror in his firm right hand and crushed it. There was no place to go, no way to run, no way to get out until his friend, darkness, arrived. He sank lower in the water and breathed through the straw, holding his nose under water.

The flames crawled higher. Everyone in the crowd waited for something and Jim didn't know what it was. The victim was dead, what more did they want from her?

As he thought about it, Jim trained his glasses on the girl's lifeless head. It was not recognizable. Just then her skull burst apart like a ripe melon from the intense pressure of the trapped boiling blood. A cheer went up from the crowd of over two hundred who watched. Three squaws jumped up and began a new wild victory dance around the disfigured body. The eldest squaw kicked the fire to one side. Then she hacked off Becky's head with her knife and set it on the rock where the fire had been. Now the three danced to an increasing tempo.

Jim turned downstream and threw up. There wasn't much in his stomach, but the dry heaves were even worse. For a minute he thought his whole stomach was coming out. He looked away from the fire circle and pushed deeper into the willows. Twice he washed out his mouth, then he drank of the clean, clear water. But Jim Steel knew that he would never be able to erase from his memory the agony of watching Becky West die.

CHAPTER TEN

Jim lay in the cold water all day keeping a careful watch for Indians who might get close. He worked out a system of kicking underwater to help keep his circulation going. He tried to do the same with his hands. He never looked back at the fire circle, and didn't see when they cut down Becky's body. They probably wouldn't bury her. The Apaches were casual about burial, for their own people as well as whites. It made little difference to them one way or another, except for their chiefs. Often an honored chief was interred with his favorite horse and dog.

When the sun came directly overhead, Jim was almost discovered, but the two boys hunting frogs along the bank and in the reeds tired of the sport fifteen yards before they could have seen him. Jim had been completely submerged, breathing only through the reed.

Once he saw brown legs through the clear water, but they stopped and went the opposite direction.

Now Jim's only thoughts were ways to stay out of sight until after dark. In the afternoon his stomach began cramping from lack of food, so he drank water every hour. It helped for a while.

When darkness came and activity around the camp slowed down, Jim crawled painfully out of the water. He knew his whole body was wrinkled up like a dried prune. He grabbed his binoculars and gun off the branches and, after a few tries, discovered he could walk.

It was well past midnight when Jim rode into the wash just below the cave where Sarah and Harry waited. He smelled smoke half a mile away and swore. When he rounded the last turn in the wash, he saw a fire burning outside the front of the cave, and a figure huddled near it.

Jim drew his six-gun and charged. Before Hamlet's hooves hit the fire, Jim saw the figure was Harry West.

'What in hell are you doing out here with a fire?' Jim roared.

Harry crouched low expecting to be hit. Jim slid off the horse and kicked Harry, rolling him into the dirt. Then Jim scattered and stomped out the last of the fire before he turned back to Harry. But the dude had picked up his blanket and scurried into the cave.

116

Jim led Hamlet into the cave and loosened the cinch. Both the other mounts had their saddles off. Then he looked for Harry. He found him whimpering beside Sarah. Jim ignored the girl's protests and dragged the man to his feet. He held Harry by his red velvet shirt front and full-arm slapped his face twice. Then Jim doubled up his right fist and knocked Harry down, hoping he'd broken his jaw.

Sarah sat and watched it. She didn't scream at him, yell, or cry. Instead she looked up and saw that some of his fury was spent.

'That's enough, Jim, don't you think? I couldn't stop him from going out there. Harry says he can't stand small places, can't stand being shut in.'

Jim stood, staring down at the tangle of arms and legs that looked like a man. 'He does something like that again and some Apache will shut him up in a grave for good. Just one wandering Chiricahua and both of you would be nothing but cold meat and bones by now, do you know that? If just one brave ran across the smell of smoke where I did . . .'

'Jim, was it very bad?'

'What?'

'The trip, into the stronghold . . . Did you find out anything?'

'If that damn brother of yours had lit that fire at just the wrong time . . .'

'Becky's dead, isn't she, Jim?'

'Yes, damnit, yes! What did you expect, and

I had to watch her die!' He was so furious at Harry that he blurted out the whole story, play by play, detail by gruesome detail before he could stop. He saw Sarah shrink down on the blanket, cringing with each new horrible fact. When he was done she sat there, her hands over her face, sobbing.

He turned and went back to Hamlet and took him for a long cool drink at the spring. He chewed on more of the dried fruit he had taken along, then drank. When he got back to the glowing fire, Sarah motioned to a small pot on the rocks.

'Want some rabbit? We've got some left.'

He nodded and she handed it to him with a fork and spoon.

She stood and her brown eyes studied him. 'Thank you for what you've done, Jim. I appreciate it. At least we know. You were right, though, we should never have found out. We'd all be better off.'

He forked a chunk of the rabbit and chewed it down, then watched her. 'I'm sorry the way I told you, I couldn't help it, that damn Harry... I shouldn't have, no call, no call at all.'

She found some hardtack for him and dug a bottle of brandy from her pack. 'It's for cooking, and medicinal purposes.' She gave it to him. Jim ate everything in sight and drank half the brandy.

Five minutes later Jim rolled his blanket and filled his saddle bags.

'Pack up,' he said. It was an order. 'We're moving out of here. We've got three hours to dawn. If we ride fast we might be able to get back to the notch in the hill before daylight. Let's move it!'

Wherever Harry was, he heard the command. Jim was surprised that Harry was the first one ready to go. Jim made sure the other two mounts had good drinks, then they killed the fire and rode out into the darkness. He had misjudged the time, they still had four hours before dawn. Now that he knew the trail, he was sure they could make it to the notch before the sun came up.

As they rode, Sarah came alongside Jim.

'I'm sorry, Jim. I never should have asked you to go in there. I didn't know what I was asking. I thought all the terrible things about Indians were made up for the dime novels. You saved my life again.'

But Jim could only nod in response, his thoughts still riled, still furious about Harry making such an outrageous blunder after he had been told.

An hour before sunup, even knowing the way, Jim saw they wouldn't make the notch before daylight. He turned up a narrow valley and stopped almost at its head in a thicket of madrona and mesquite and a scattering of young pines with branches low to the ground. It made a perfect screen. They tied the horses, loosened the cinches, and rolled out blankets.

It would be daylight soon.

'No fires, no food, no noise, just some sleep,' Jim said. 'And be sure that nobody goes outside this screen of brush when it's daylight. We don't know how many Chiricahua there might be beating this brush for game.'

Jim stretched out on his blanket. He had gone to sleep once in the saddle, but the other two hadn't noticed. He yawned and tried to think how long it had been since he'd slept. Two days, sixty hours? He couldn't remember. Their security here was better than it could have been on the desert. He dropped off to sleep at once.

It was full daylight as Harry West woke and lay on his blanket thinking about Philadelphia. He had friends there, important friends. He'd never been kicked and pushed around so much in his life as in the last week. Not that a little beating was all bad, if the man had good intentions. But anger, that was bad. He was pleased that they were heading back. Two days, maybe three, and he could spend hours in a hot tub. Then at least he could demand that they go back to civilization, back to Philadelphia!

He sat up, staring at Jim, but not moving toward him. Jim wasn't one of the club, and never would be. Harry sighed, he had such a fine-looking, strong body. He saw that Sarah was sleeping now, too. He would never forgive her for dragging him along on this fool's

120

errand. It had been madness from the start, and he should have simply refused to go ... only he knew she would have stamped her foot, scolded him about being a man, and left on her own.

He rubbed his crotch, and stood. He had to urinate and he wasn't going to do it where Jim might see him. It wouldn't hurt to step through the brush for just a minute. He went fifty feet away from the others, past the pines to a larger tree and relieved himself. On the way back he stepped on a dead branch and it snapped in half with a loud crack and tripped him. He swore out loud as he fell and gave a little cry.

Harry sat up and rubbed his ankle, then looked in front of him. Fifty feet away he saw an Indian standing beside a pine tree. He wore nothing but cut-off pants. His face was scowling and his bow was pulled to its maximum. Harry clawed for the gun on his belt. He knew how to use it. His father made sure he could shoot a pistol even before he climaxed the first time. Harry stared in terror as the arrow released before his gun came up.

But the arrow, one of the willow reeds from the stronghold, had not dried straight and took a wild turn just after it left the bow. Harry fired the six-gun, but at fifty feet he missed. The Indian's second arrow darted on its way shortly after Harry had fired.

The arrow flew straight and true, its duck-feathered tip homing in perfectly on Harry's belly. The two-inch-wide, three-inch-long obsidian arrowhead plunged in deep, slicing through intestines and other vital organs, lodging its tip against his spine.

Harry sat down suddenly, the gun still in his hand. He knew he was hurt bad. But he fired again, and saw the round slant through the Chiricahua's neck, spinning him backward. Harry fired three more times, watching the slugs smash into the Indian's body. Then Harry looked down at the arrow shaft protruding from his belly and cried out softly as he toppled backward.

Jim came to his feet, his gun in hand, when the first shot ripped through the idyllic calm of the mountain. He ran toward the sound and before the last shot echoed away, he came up behind Harry. Jim saw Harry down with the arrow in him, scanned the area ahead, and spotted the Chiricahua. With his gun cocked he approached the red man and made certain he was dead. Then he ran back to Harry.

'Harry, you got him. The Indian's dead. How do you feel?'

'Terrible!' Harry began to cry. 'I'm all cut up inside, I know it. I've seen those big arrowheads.' He cried again.

Sarah ran up, saw what had happened, and crossed herself. She looked at Jim. He shook his head. There was no chance for the boy now, not gut shot with a big arrow. She took Harry's head in her lap and began talking to him. She spoke about all the good times they had had.

Jim checked the quiver on the Indian. The arrowheads were the big ones, for killing deer. He came back and listened to Sarah.

'And then we'll take Dad to Philadelphia with us. You can go back to work in the bank, just like you used to. It will all come out fine.'

'No,' Harry said. 'I'm not going anywhere.' He gasped as a sheet of pain stabbed through him. 'I know what's happening. I'm dying. Just take care of Dad for me. He's getting old.' Harry coughed and blood came from his mouth. Sarah wiped it away.

'Sarah, I'm sorry for all the trouble I caused you. I didn't try to be ... to be different.'

'Harry, you're fine, you're just perfect! Now don't worry about anything. We'll get you on your horse and in no time at all we'll be back in Tucson where they have good doctors.'

Harry was still looking at her, but his eyes didn't move. He wasn't seeing anything. He hadn't coughed, or cried out, or moaned; he simply died in her arms as she talked to him.

Jim reached over and closed Harry's eyelids, moved him out of Sarah's lap, and helped her stand. He couldn't let her go into shock, they didn't have time.

'Sarah, there were five shots, remember? We don't have much time. Go get his horse.' Sarah heard him, but looked up, puzzled.

He slapped her gently. 'Sarah, go get Harry's horse, right now!'

She jumped, blinked, then ran for his mount.

Jim took Harry's gun and put it back in his hand, forcing his fingers around the grip. Then he backed away and looked at the scene. It should do. He took the horse from Sarah when she came and looped the reins around some brush ten feet from Harry's body.

'Sarah, you know we can't bury him. We have to leave him here so the Chiricahuas can find him.'

Her eyes went wild for a moment, as anger and fury slanted across her face.

'Sarah, if they find a dead brave here where the shots came from, they'll look for who did it. If they find Harry, too, they'll figure he killed the Indian, so they won't search. The brave will take his horse back to the stronghold along with his gun and pack. Harry is buying us time to get out of here.'

She nodded, and he wondered if she really understood. They didn't have time to talk about it then. Five or six Indians were probably already moving quickly toward them. He got her back on her black and they rode. Twice they moved up canyons, then over ridges until they came to another stand of small pines and brush that would hide them. They left their mounts saddled and ready to ride, then lay down on a carpet of pine needles to watch and wait.

Jim had selected a position where he could see one of the trails that led back to the

124

stronghold. He watched it. It was well past midday when he spotted two horses moving slowly up the ridge. With his binoculars he saw the second mount had two bodies tied over the saddle. Harry West was going to the stronghold after all. Jim decided he wouldn't tell Sarah, at least not right then.

Jim had worried about being followed to this hideout from the death scene. He had taken several routes over rocky footing to forestall just that. If the brave who got there first was satisfied that it was a one-to-one killing, he would be eager to return home with the prize and claim the big strong white-eye's horse, his pistol, and saddle.

Sarah had not been sleeping.

'Jim, I feel so bad, like a barbarian, not giving Harry a decent Christian burial.'

He moved closer to her. 'I know, Sarah, I'm sorry too.'

'But he did disobey orders, he was well outside of our screen,' Sarah said.

Jim scratched his growing beard, wishing now that he had taken time to shave. 'I've been thinking that Harry might just have saved us. That Indian might have seen us ride in. He may have been moving up on us, hoping to kill us all as we slept.'

Sarah began to cry. 'Then Harry saved us, instead of making more trouble?'

Jim nodded.

Her grief poured out then and she fell

against him, needing his support. Jim's arms came around her and held her as she sobbed. She was small and so fragile, crying her heart out for two deaths in her family within the span of twenty-four hours. It took her fifteen minutes to sob out her sadness. Then she wiped her eyes and pushed away from him.

'I guess I'm not so tough after all, not so self sufficient.'

'You're doing just fine.' She had something else on her mind. Jim waited for her. He watched a red ant carrying a large white maggot on its back. It had stopped in front of a foot-high rock and Jim made a bet with himself the ant would go around the rock, not over it. It hesitated, then crawled up and over the rock.

'Jim, what about two horses, and two people? Could we go on through the middle of Chiricahua country as easily as one?'

'No.'

'But if you had to take me all the way to Tucson, and then work your way back to this point, that would be at least six more days of exposing yourself to the Apaches that you really wouldn't have to, right?'

He nodded.

'So it would be safer for you to move on from here to whatever gold mine you're going after.'

Jim hesitated for just the flutter of an eyebrow and she sensed it.

'I'm right, Jim. You know I am. I can take

126

care of myself on the trail. I won't cause you any trouble. I can build a smokeless fire and skin a rabbit. I wouldn't feel right making you put in six more days of unnecessary exposure to the Chiricahua if you don't have to. And you certainly don't.'

Jim stared at her. It was a decision he wished he didn't have to make. Should he push on to the wall of gold now, or should he take Sarah to safety, and not move ahead from this point for at least six more days?

CHAPTER ELEVEN

He looked away from the girl and toward the trail where her brother had just been carried head-down. Sure, she asked to go along, but did he have the *right* to take her deeper into trouble? Hadn't he done enough to her family already? Damnit, he hadn't invited them to follow him. But it would be six days before he could move on. It seemed like a six-year sentence. He figured they had now penetrated one half of the way to the wall of gold.

Jim made up his mind. Slowly he nodded. 'All right, we'll move ahead, but you'll do exactly what I say, especially on safety and security. I've seen enough of the West family killed for one trip.'

'Thank you, Jim.' She hesitated, and looked

up at the same trail he had scanned. 'Now, hadn't you better be getting some sleep? I'll stand guard.'

Jim watched her, hoping she was steady again, reliable. She was making good sense. 'Look, Sarah. I'm still not happy about this. This is one-man-sneak-through country. Two bodies and two horses make it four times as dangerous. You still sure you want to go along?'

'Yes, you're stuck with me. No easy way to get rid of me now. And I know you won't send me back alone. Don't fight the problem, Captain, just carry on.' She was grinning as she said it, but he detected a new note of hardness in her voice.

It wasn't the old army lingo that clued him to her change. Jim nodded, stretched out on the pine needle mulch and closed his eyes. A new element had entered, something neither of them had thought about before, but now she remembered and it changed her whole attitude. Now it was her honor, her female body she was worried about. Suddenly she was concerned about propriety! Jim snorted. That was it, had to be. He could set her mind at rest about that point. He was looking for gold, not an unwilling girl. Jim wondered if he should say it, right then; put her at her ease? He decided against it. Let her find out the slow way, let her worry a little. He'd been doing enough worrying about and because of her and her kin in the past three days. He smiled, relaxed, and went to sleep.

Sarah sat there on the pine needles and leaves wondering what was going to happen to her. Yes, true, she had brought it all on herself. She had insisted on coming out here to rescue Becky. Harry's death was her fault too. Tears brimmed her eyes, but she swept them away. Both Becky and Harry gone! She could still scarcely believe it. They both had been so young to die.

And why in heaven's name did she insist on Jim continuing his little prospecting trip? She could have been back in Tucson in three days—instead of heading deeper into the wild and dangerous hostile Indian country. Why?

She swept her eyes around the countryside, what little of it she could see through the screen of brush. Did her decision come in part because he was such an attractive man? Was it because he was strong and sure of himself, swift-acting, dominant, yet with the capacity for tenderness; in short, because he was twice the man in every way that her short-time husband had been?

Sarah closed her eyes. She wondered if her sudden change in mood had caught his attention. It must have. She simply couldn't help it. A dozen years of being told what nice girls do and don't do, and how to act properly around men—you don't throw that off in a moment. When she realized fully that Harry was dead, and they were gone from him, she understood that she was alone with Jim, alone in the wilderness, and he could take her if he wished. In the past she hadn't been properly reserved with him. And of course that impulsive, silly time in the stable when she practically invited him to seduce her.

Sarah sighed. She simply had to put him on notice that she wasn't someone he could walk all over if he wanted to. Although she had to admit that he certainly hadn't made any improper advances toward her. In fact he had made none at all. She had noticed hardly a flicker from him that he knew she was a woman. But now that the immediate Indian danger was lessened...

She dozed. She had no idea how long she had slept, but when she woke it was with a start. She looked at Jim to see if he was awake, if he had noticed. She breathed again when she saw him sleeping. He had been awake for so long, she didn't see how he could still ride a horse. Two and half days he was without sleep, and all because she had asked, urged, pleaded for him to go find Becky.

But what now? There would be many lonely nights of travel, and lonely days hiding, hovering over a small fire, being thrown together. She would be calm and cool. She would set the tone, not give him a chance to misinterpret her actions. She would keep him on the defensive if need be. And she would be so efficient, so good on the trail and in camp about security and quietness and hiding that he wouldn't have a chance to critize her. Yes, that should do it. She would not give him any reason to think of her as a woman, to desire her body.

Sarah watched the sun. It was rimming the far edge of the mountains. In an hour it would be dusk. She looked at Jim, lying on his side, as relaxed as a big cougar. His right hand lay an inch from his loaded six-gun. She didn't understand what was so appealing about him. He was so different from the officers she had known at the forts, and of course from her husband. She shouldn't be thinking this way.

'Jim, Jim, time to wake up.' She blushed the moment she said it, she sounded like a wife! 'Jim, rise and shine. Hit the deck. Come on you strawfoot, get moving!' Her voice rose as she barked out the cleaned up version of the old army sergeant's morning call.

Jim sat up. His hand brushed the .44 and eased it back into its holster, tied down to his thick thigh. 'I wondered if you remembered the whole thing. You know what a strawfoot is?'

'Of course. During the war the farm boys couldn't tell their right foot from their left. But they knew straw from hay, so the sergeants tied straw to one of their feet and called out, "strawfoot, hayfoot," instead of right and left.'

'You're an army kid, that's for certain,' Jim said.

'It'll also be dark in an hour, Jim. You know

which way we're moving out of here?'

'Near enough. How are we on food?'

'I put some of our food in Harry's ...' She stopped. 'In the other saddlebag. Maybe we have enough left for two days. If we eat light.'

'Yeah, about what I figured. I been gettin' too fat lately anyhow.' He went to his saddlebags and brought back a flat slab of jerky. With the big Case knife he cut off two slices, and handed her one. 'It ain't the Philadelphia Carriage House restaurant, but it'll keep us moving. What you don't eat now, put in your pocket. Taste mighty good about midnight.'

He brought some of the dried fruit and the canteens and they ate the fruit, then chewed on the jerky.

'I guess you read in the newspaper about Seward's Folly,' she said. 'The big icebox that William Seward bought called Alaska, for seven million dollars.'

'Nope, hadn't got around to that one. What do we want with Alaska?'

'He says it's a bargain. Just wish that big icebox were here right now and full of food.'

'Wouldn't hurt my feelings. We better get packing.' She was on her feet a half-second behind him, and had her black ready to ride before Jim was prepared. He looked at her with no expression whatsoever.

'That gun loaded?' he asked. She wore on her belt a small caliber six-gun with a short barrel.

'Of course.'

'Unload it. Put the shells in your pocket.'

'What good is it then? I don't . . .'

His blue eyes stabbed into her brown ones and held them.

'So we don't have another accidental discharge of a weapon,' she said, understanding.

'If you need that little gun, we'll have plenty of warning, and plenty of time for you to load it.'

She pushed the rounds out of the weapon and put them in her jacket pocket.

'We'll be winding around the side of the mountain where the stronghold sits, so keep a sharp eye. You get the rear guard position. We'll travel steady, making as much distance as we can each night, from first dusk to first light. Be easy to find a place to hole up with all this brush. Can you take it?'

This time she stared at him until he looked away.

They began moving. Jim wasn't sure where he had landed at the end of his frantic half-hour's ride after Harry got killed. Now he made it to a ridge while it was still partly dusk and oriented himself against the blue-tinged lines and peaks. His mental map picture came back into focus and he moved out, heading generally south and east again, hoping to skirt the big mountain by at least five miles and keep away from most of the Chiricahua hunters.

They rested just past midnight and ate the rest of the hardtack and the last can of beans from his pack. Jim settled back against a pine enjoying the food. He wouldn't see beans for at least a week, so he wanted to remember how they tasted. They had talked little on the ride since there was no reason and few chances. Now neither of them spoke. Even though the night was mild, he noticed how she kept her jacket buttoned to her neck. She was suddenly shy, afraid of him. That was a big switch from her dance hall act in the stable.

'Are you sure you know where you're going?' she asked.

'Hell, yes.'

'You don't have to swear.'

'You don't have to ask dumb questions.'

'Sorry you brought me along?'

'Of course.'

'Where are we going?'

'You don't need to know.'

'I want to know.'

'That wasn't in our agreement.'

'Damn the agreement!' she said.

'You don't have to swear.' Jim waited for her to react, but she said nothing more. 'Now that you've got that out of your craw, what's really troubling you?'

'Nothing. Not a thing. I watch my brother die, I find out my only sister has been tortured to death by savages, I'm on a sneaky trip

134

through hostile Indian country with a man who snaps, yells, and swears at me. Why should there be anything troubling me?'

'It was your idea to come ahead.'

'Sure, it's all my fault!'

Jim left the tree and checked the horses. Both were grazing, looking for water. When he came back she sat up and scowled at him through the darkness.

'Do you always run away from a fight?'

'Yes, ma'am, when it's with a woman.'

'Think of me as just another trail hand. Where are we going?'

Jim let her question hang in the air, until she stirred where she sat and almost spoke. What could it hurt?

'I'm looking for a wall of gold, a gold mine of the Apache nation.'

'We're on a lost gold mine, wild goose chase?'

'No, it's real. I know about it because of an honor-debt. But if you don't believe it, you can turn around and try to find your way out of here anytime you want to.'

She stood now, anger shooting from every pore. 'I'm sorry if I insulted you. I guess I made a mistake and thought you might be halfway human. I was wrong.'

Jim cinched the saddle on his horse and stowed the last of the food things. He swung aboard Hamlet, not waiting to see if she came or not. She stared after him for a moment, then set her jaw and followed.

Jim found what he was hunting for just before dawn, the looming twin peaks, the sheep's horns Swift Hawk had told him about. He stopped the horses and searched a moment, then rode into a small ravine choked with brush. It would make an ideal spot to hide during the daylight hours. As he started a small smokeless fire, Sarah got out coffee and water. She seemed in better spirits now. Jim didn't even remember what they had quarreled about, but he wasn't going to apologize. She was an unexpected and unwelcome nuisance on this trip. He took his bow and arrows and told her he'd be right back.

Jim spent an hour hunting for a rabbit. He had two shots and missed them both. He retrieved the arrows and walked back to camp, where he dug out the last of the dried fruit. They had passed a small stream earlier and had watered the horses and filled their canteens.

'How much farther?' she asked.

'Two, maybe three days.'

'And then all the way back?'

'Nope, we'll keep on going and come out near Tombstone.'

'Oh,' she said, then went on chewing on a dried apricot.

They rolled out blankets, and Jim saw that she put hers on the far side of the horses. He hadn't planned on going to sleep right away. He thought he'd wait until the sun came up, but he couldn't hold off. He felt safer in this brush than he had for days. And he hadn't seen any sign of Chiricahua hunters around here. The wall of gold seemed within reach.

Jim woke up and saw the sun almost overhead. He had slept for six hours. He lifted up and checked on Sarah, then jumped to his feet. She wasn't lying where she had been. He ran past Hamlet and saw that both Sarah and her black were gone. She must have taken seriously his idea of her turning around and riding for Tucson. She was out there somewhere alone, and riding in the daylight!

CHAPTER TWELVE

Jim had Hamlet ready to ride in thirty seconds, but before he mounted he knelt and studied the hoof prints of the black. The prints were light, not even Sarah's hundred pounds showed in the marks left in the soft earth. So Sarah had led the black down the ravine and away from camp. He guessed she would follow form, she would do a backtracking job on the trail they had ridden in the previous night. Jim spurred Hamlet up the side of the ravine. Sarah would be moving down the canyon, then she'd make a swing to the right. He could go up the ridge and maybe spot her from on top. Jim had no idea when she had left. It had been six that morning

137

when he lay down. Jim hoped she hadn't left with a six-hour head start on him.

At the top of the first ridge he stopped and pulled up the army field glasses. This was still high pine country, partially covered with virgin trees. There was spotty brush in the ravines, but not much on the slopes. Jim began sweeping the long valley in front of him in the time-tested double-grid method. On the sixth cross pattern, he spotted movement in the shadows of some pines. Concentrating on the point, Jim watched a pair of deer walk into the open country. He went back to sectionalizing the valley and the slopes. Ten minutes later he put down the glasses and rubbed his eyes. She could be ten miles away by now, with a Chiricahua about to lift her scalp.

Jim pushed the glasses up and worked the whole valley again. Not far from where he had seen the deer, Jim found movement again, only this time he spotted a horse and rider moving through the patterns of shade along the side of the valley, utilizing the best cover available. The horse was a black. He checked the lay of the land remembering how they had come into the big valley last night. She would swing down the flat to the end and turn right again, if she were still backtracking—and that's the only map she had. Knowing Sarah as much as he did, Jim guessed she would be following the trail they had made.

Jim pictured the area in his mind. If he could

138

cut across the valley, and up the far ridge, then down the other side, he should be able to get to the trail before she did, and drop right down in front of her. The only problem was he'd have to ride through wide-open country, inviting any Chiricahua in the area to come in and make a try for his scalp. He watched her riding farther away and made up his mind, spurring Hamlet down the other side of the ridge and toward the valley below.

He rode hard, and felt the big buckskin respond, with only one sidelong glance to be sure he was doing what Jim wanted. They jolted down the slope, then sprinted the half-mile across the valley. Each moment Jim wondered if he would catch a surprise arrow in the chest or stir up a hornet's nest of Indians. But he made it to the far side and began walking up the slope through the trees. This ridge line was higher, and it took him twenty minutes to ride to the top. When he got there he swung down off Hamlet and took out the glasses.

His estimation of the distance to the end of the finger ridge was about a mile and a half. He spotted nothing through the binoculars. He looked over the valley and saw it was much like the other, a sprinkling of trees on the now-dry hills and grass in the valley floor. Be good grazing land for a few months. These valleys all seemed to lead into one another like branches of a stream going into a river. He was sure

Sarah would come this way, working back down the trail they had marked out the night before. He guessed she'd be on the near side of the valley floor, moving in and out along the edge of the timber. He began riding again, down the incline, careful now to stay in the shade and under the trees as much as possible. Halfway down he pulled up again and watched the far slopes, and then the trail where he figured Sarah would come. He saw nothing.

Along here they had ridden last night near the timber at the left of the valley, and he guessed that Sarah would do the same. Jim scanned the rest of the broad expanse of grass, hunting for a dust trail, a thread of smoke, movement, any sign of hostiles. He found nothing.

Jim worked lower on the slope, staying in the heavier wooded section now, coming down to within ten yards of the valley floor. He settled behind a pair of young pines and checked the countryside once more. At last he could spot movement far ahead on the near side of the valley. Soon he could tell through the glasses that it was a black horse, and the tilt of a small hat tied it down: it was Sarah.

As he waited, he scanned the rest of the valley, working across the floor toward the far timber over half a mile away. There was no movement, but Jim's glasses paused and held on one clump of brush near the outlet of a dry wash at the edge of the timber. It seemed to have an excessively thick section. He watched it closer and saw motion, like a horse sawing its head up and down impatiently.

'An Indian,' Jim said softly. Hamlet pricked up his ears, turned his head. Jim patted his neck, rubbing it down as he watched with the glasses. He looked back at Sarah who was making slow progress, trying not to kick up any dust, staying in the shadows. Jim estimated the Indian was nearly the same distance from Sarah as he was, three-quarters of a mile. But Jim was only half a mile from the hostile. Had the Indian spotted Jim? Could he fade down through the timber and get closer to Sarah before there was an attack? He assumed there was one brave, but there could be four or six in there. Jim paused, trying to decide his best strategy. There was no company commander to consult here. He was on his own.

As Jim checked the Indian behind the brush, the decision was made for him. One, then two braves charged from the brush on sleek, army-fed horses, riding full gallop for Sarah. Jim didn't waste any time on the glasses now, he kicked Hamlet in the flanks and jolted from his cover into the grassy valley floor, angling toward the path of the Chiricahuas, to cut them off before they got to Sarah.

He couldn't risk using the rifle, or pistol. It had to be done quietly. Jim kept Hamlet running hard, making it half way to the natives before they saw him. They veered toward him, both drawing arrows. Jim leaned down close along the buckskin's neck and heard arrows flying past. He drew his big knife and closed in, watching for them to separate. But they didn't have a chance to mousetrap him. One of the brown horses hit a gopher hole, snapping a leg bone, tumbling the rider off the mount straight toward Jim. Jim angled Hamlet into the crawling Indian, riding him down, feeling the big horse's hooves contacting flesh. Then he was past and wheeling around, charging toward the other brave who had changed directions and was rushing toward Sarah. Hamlet's reserve power surpassed the Indian's mount, but there wasn't time to make up the distance. The Chiricahua came at Sarah as she walked the black out of a patch of pines, unaware of the danger.

When the brave saw she was a woman, he let out a war whoop which stopped Sarah motionless. The brave bore down, swept her from her saddle, but in the tussle he lost his balance and both tumbled off the bareback horse. Jim rode into the area thirty seconds later and saw Sarah stumbling away and the Indian sitting up shaking his head to clear it. Jim rode at him, came off in a half-dive like he was bulldogging a cantankerous calf and they both rolled into the sandy grass. Jim lost his hold on the Chiricahua and came up with his big Case fighting knife in his hand.

The other had out his knife now, too, and he

142

circled Jim, looking first at him, then at the girl. Jim drove in, slashing with the heavy blade, testing the ability of the red man. The Indian jumped back out of the way, and made a feint, then drew back. Both slashed and slashed again, trying for that one chance to move in and cut or kill.

The Indian was a good knife-fighter, and only the heavier blade Jim had and its eight-inch length kept him in the battle. The red man parried the thrusts, waited his chance, and drove in expertly at each opening.

Jim began to feel the weight of the big blade. He tried a new approach, a head-on charge that would bring the other's knife up as a defense. He moved forward now, working the Indian backward until he had the knife where he wanted it, and then he charged in, his big blade slashing down with authority.

The Chiricahua thrust his own weapon up to block it, but the weight and force of the larger blade tore the red man's knife from his hand.

The brave jumped back, unarmed, surprised. He moved quickly, gaining a few steps, jumping back from the heavy blade's slashes. Jim drove in relentlessly, knowing what he had to do, hoping now it would be easier. But the red man found a limb from a pine tree, three feet long and as big as his wrist. He grabbed it and used it to attack, driving Jim backward. Jim lost track of Sarah, and found he was being moved to the rear and to his left.

He didn't understand the tactic.

The Indian seemed content only to force Jim backwards. He glanced over his shoulder to check the area for any logs or holes, and saw the reason for the strategy. The first Indian Jim had ridden down was limping toward him, now only a dozen yards away. His arm swept back and threw a knife. Jim dodged to one side, then turned and raced toward the injured brave and drove the knife into his belly. Before Jim could withdraw the blade, the red man twisted to one side, taking the deathly instrument with him.

Jim jumped back, watching for the first Indian. He had vanished. Jim knew that was impossible. He had to be within ten yards of him. Jim checked the ground carefully. They had been fighting in an area of tough flat grass and rough brown sandy soil. He could see his footprints through it. He checked again and noticed a bulge in the landscape, and he saw him. The Indian lay in a sandy area and had covered his body with the brown sand until he almost did vanish into the background. Before he could jump up and swing his club, Jim lunged on top of him, kicking him hard in the side, dropping with his knees on the brave's heaving chest. They rolled over in the brown sand, Jim outweighing the other by forty pounds, each fighting desperately for some hold. At last Jim raised up and smashed his fist into the Chiricahua's throat, stunning him. Jim grabbed his neck with both hands and

144

squeezed, trying to choke him.

Jim watched the man's face as his eyes bulged and the pupils rolled up out of sight. He counted the slow pulses on the red man's temple and heard rasping gasps for breath through the smashed and closing windpipe. The brave's arms flailed at him, pounding him with strong blows, but they grew weaker and weaker. Jim held the throat tightly. He was worried about a fake. He held the grip another two minutes, until he saw no pulse at all at the temple, and heard no kind of a sound from the Indian's nose or mouth. Then he jumped back and pulled his six-gun, as he checked the brave.

He was dead.

Jim sighed and went to the other Chiricahua, took his knife from the belly and wiped the blood away on the grass. Only then did he turn to look for Sarah, and Hamlet. Hamlet grazed a dozen yards away. One of the Indian ponies stood, head down, waiting. The other beast thrashed on the ground with a broken leg. Jim ran over and slashed the injured horse's throat, making quick end to what otherwise would have been a long, painful death.

Then he ran to Sarah where she sat on a mound of grass near Hamlet. He still breathed hard from the physical and emotional drain of the fight. Sarah cried silently as he came up. She held her left elbow, and did not move her left shoulder at all.

'Your arm, Sarah, is it broken?'

'Jim! Oh, Jim, I'm so glad to see you. I was a silly fool, I'm sorry, I shouldn't have run off like a ninny. I apologize, and I'm sorry I made you come find me ... rescue me ... again.'

He nodded, trying to get her calmed down. 'Don't worry about that, what about your elbow?'

'I don't think it's broken, but I can't move my shoulder.'

Jim knelt in front of her, and touched her shoulder tenderly. The upper arm seemed whole, but on top of the shoulder he found a raised roundish hump.

'Hurt a lot?'

'Yes, especially when I try to move it. I hit on my shoulder when I fell from that horse.'

Jim felt it again. The shoulder was dislocated, the bone had jumped out of the socket. He had seen several of them before.

'Sarah, it isn't as serious as it feels. I think it's dislocated, your arm popped out of the shoulder joint when you hit the ground. And that was a smart move falling off that pony or I'd still be chasing you. You'll have to tell me how you got away from him.'

'I bit him.'

Jim laughed, it seemed to drain some of the tension out of him, and from her too. Jim sat down beside her.

'I'm going to have to pop that arm back in place. It's going to hurt a lot for just a minute, then it should feel better.'

She watched him, her eyes wary. 'You really know what you're doing?'

'Yes, I've done it before.'

She sighed. 'It couldn't hurt any worse than it does now.'

He turned toward her, put his foot carefully against her arm pit, and took her upper arm in both his hands. He pulled forward gently.

Sarah groaned, then cried out in pain. He continued the pressure and pulled harder, and harder still. Sarah screamed in torment. All at once the arm jumped, popping back in place, and Sarah stopped crying. He took his foot away.

'That feel better?'

She brushed away the tears and looked at him, then lifted her arm and smiled. 'Oh, yes, marvelous! How in the world did you learn to do that?'

'Just a little wild West make-do medicine. Your arm is going to be stiff and sore for a few days, but you can use it and ride and even carry firewood. In a week it should be back to normal.'

'Thanks, Jim, again. It seems ...' She stopped and looked toward the one Indian she could see. 'The other Chiricahua?'

'Both of them are past caring what we do.'

'Both dead?'

He nodded.

'Well, it seems you're still at it, getting the stupid West family out of trouble.'

'One out of three isn't a very good record.'

'Jim, I meant what I said. I'm sorry that I ran away. It was just stupid, a woman ninny thing to do, and I feel terrible. I just couldn't stand it anymore. I mean with Harry gone, and us alone ... I mean I felt so alone, so vulnerable, I guess. And after I'd badgered you into helping me ...'

'I haven't made any complaints. You've done better on the trail than any woman I know could have.'

'But I shamed you into helping me, into taking risks I had no right to ask of you. And when it was over I acted like a schoolgirl afraid of a man, afraid of her first kiss.'

'Are you still afraid?'

She watched him without speaking, a soft smile on her face.

He moved closer beside her and kissed her lips gently. Sarah sighed and leaned back. 'That wasn't anything to be afraid of, was it?' She leaned forward and kissed him, her arms going around his neck. When they parted she smiled.

'Sarah, I can't tell you what to do. But that invitation is still open to ride on to Tombstone with me. I really hope you'll want to come along.'

CHAPTER THIRTEEN

'Good, Jim, because I do want to go. I'll do my part this time, I promise. You won't have to worry about me.'

Jim studied her pretty face, saw the concerned smile there, and sensed her shift in attitude again. Before she had turned cold, hard, but now she seemed relaxed with a feeling of contentment, even softness coming through. He smiled and nodded.

'Good, Jim, it will work out.'

He looked at the braves' bodies. There was no time now to bury them, and how could he get rid of the horse even if he did get the Indians in the ground? There was no chance.

'We'd better get out of here and under some cover. Hard telling how many more Chiricahuas are watching us right now.' He caught the black horse, which had wandered off, and helped Sarah mount. As soon as he swung up on Hamlet, they rode into the trees at the near side of the valley. Once in the shade and, Jim hoped, out of sight, he leaned up against a pine tree and lifted the binoculars. Systematically he combed the valley and the slopes, but could find no more sign of Indians.

'Let's hope they were a casual pair of hunters, and not part of a larger group,' Jim said. 'Now we better find ourselves a good hole to crawl into until dark.'

He found the spot half a mile ahead. They moved up and over the ridge and down the far side. He rode Hamlet forward, forcing his way into a thicket of chaparral brush in a small canyon. Inside the screen he found a tiny clearing and they both dismounted and tied the horses. Jim slashed away some of the brush and they sat down.

'How's the shoulder?'

She smiled at that. Here they were liable to be scalped at any moment and he asked about her sore shoulder. 'It's better. Oh, it hurts a little now and then, but it's great considering how it felt an hour ago. Thanks again.'

'Welcome. Now you stay put, get some sleep if you can. I'm going to try to sharpen up my bow and arrow work on some unsuspecting rabbits.'

A hundred yards from their little camp, Jim shot the first rabbit, but broke an arrow doing it. He got a second rabbit on the way back ten minutes later. At once he gutted both animals, and skinned one, burying the offal under leaf mold. Then he slipped back into the camp. He decided to risk a small fire.

'If some redskin spots those bodies down there, they got to know somebody's around here close. One little smokeless fire can't hurt all that much.'

'Besides, you're getting hungry for something more than dried prunes and water,'

Sarah said, grinning.

They roasted the rabbit, cutting it into pieces and cooking it over the flames on the end of two green sticks. When Sarah had eaten all she wanted, Jim finished up the last three pieces, throwing the bones into the brush.

'Some of those pan-fried biscuits of yours sure would have tasted good with that,' Jim said.

'Next time I'll plan better.'

She watched him bury the fire with dry dirt to stop it from smoking. 'I wish it were dark,' Sarah said. 'Then we could get moving. You sure there's a real wall of gold out there?'

'When an old Indian is dying, and you do him a favor, he doesn't make up a wild story just to amuse himself. It's a matter of honor. The Life-giver would be furious with a Chiricahua who lied on his deathbed.'

She stretched out on her blanket, favoring her left shoulder.

'Did you get much sleep last night?'

Sarah shook her head.

'I can't figure out why. You better sleep now.'

'Is that an order, Captain?'

'At ease, Corporal. Anyway, I was only a first lieutenant.'

Sarah saluted and laughed. 'And a civilian at heart all the way, I bet. Well, thanks, civilian, for fixing my arm.'

'Welcome. Anything else you need right

now?'

'Yes, a bath.'

He sloshed his canteen. 'I don't think I have enough left.'

She turned over and tried to sleep. Jim was too keyed up to drop off. He lay on his blanket and went on continual guard duty. The two bodies in the open valley still bothered him. But there was no way to hide them without spending hours there. Those hours would have kept them in the open, subject to discovery from a thousand spots. Buzzards were probably already circling, or eating. With luck the birds would strip the bodies before any other Indian found them. That way the knife death would not show, and it could be put down to lack of water or an accident. The dead horse would help that idea.

Jim looked around again, saw a rabbit scamper past. He knew they shouldn't be here, shouldn't have stopped so close to the valley with the bodies, but he was trapped. This was simply the less risky of his options. A calculated risk they had to take. At least it was better than digging under the bodies or traveling by daylight.

He lay there, his chin propped on his elbows, looking through the brush and listening.

Once a covey of quail burst up from the open forest a few yards away. It glued Jim to his position for ten minutes, but he saw nothing that could have scared them. Maybe they just decided to move. It wasn't a Chiricahua sneaking up on them, he was sure of that.

At dusk, he roused her. They each ate an apricot half he found in his saddlebag and drank some water from low canteens. When they could see no more than a hundred feet, they rode out, down the rest of the slope and across the valley back to the trail Jim had laid out the night before.

Jim pushed hard. It was just after midnight, when they wound past another flank of the tall mountain and dropped down into a valley, when Jim called a halt. They were next to a small creek that they could jump across. The water bubbled down from some high springs and coursed over sand and pebbles.

The horses drank first. Then they drank, and refilled their canteens.

Sarah looked up, water still dripping from her nose.

'Oh, Jim. Do we have time for me to take a bath? I even brought some soap and a towel.'

'Bath? Where?'

'Right here, in the stream. I'm so gritty I feel like sandpaper. Please Jim. It won't take me long.'

'And you want me to ride into the brush somewhere?'

She stood very near to him. Suddenly she reached around his neck and stretched up and kissed his lips, feeling the mustache tickle her nose. She pushed her breasts tightly against his chest. When she let go she smiled. 'Jim, you don't have to ride off anywhere. The fact is, I was hoping that you'd scrub my back.'

Jim's arms had come around her and he held her against him.

'Sarah, you don't have to do this. I didn't put any conditions on helping you.'

'I don't have to do what? All I said was I wanted you to ...'

'Sarah. You don't have to. You're the prettiest thing I've seen in six states. Any man in his right mind would ride a dozen days just to get a look at you. But you still don't have to.'

She kissed him again, then loosened his hands, and unbuttoned her jacket. 'Jim, I know I don't have to.' She caught his hand and brought it to her breast. 'Jim, I want to.'

The water was cold as they sat on the edge of the little creek. Using half the towel they scrubbed each other in the moonlight until their skin glistened. Jim washed her back, then they dried themselves and stretched out on the double thickness of both blankets.

At first they explored, and whispered and laughed softly. Then they made love in the filtered light, joining in a tender union that swept over and consumed both of them.

A half hour later she leaned over him, her bare breasts brushing his chest as she kissed him. 'Jim, hadn't we better put a few more miles under those hooves tonight?'

Jim stirred in a half sleep and pulled her

154

down, kissing her contentedly. Then they sat up.

'Yes, Sergeant, I think you're right,' he said.

'Hey, I just got promoted.'

They dressed. Jim checked the terrain, and they rode again. They were veering more south here, moving around the stronghold.

Only two hours after they stopped at the creek, Jim halted in front of her. Ahead he could see a campfire. That could mean only one thing, an Indian encampment of some kind. He left the horses with her and moved up quietly, so cautiously that he spotted one lookout and went around him before he could get close enough to see the camp. It was a fair-sized stream, but there were no permanent buildings or wickiups. The group of about twenty adults seemed to be sleeping around fires. He counted blankets, then strained to see what hung in the trees. At last he spotted the long strips of meat, venison. They must be making jerky here, and taking the finished goods back to the stronghold. To confirm this idea he saw two big buck deer hanging up to cool out.

Jim crawled back to the horses twice as cautiously as he had approached the campsite. He headed the mounts back down the trail he had come and circled around the camp by more than a mile.

It was unusual to have a special hunting camp. Jim dismissed it, glad that they were past the danger spot. He wanted to be as far away as possible from it by daylight, before the hunters spread out from their blankets with first light, like honeybees after clover.

As they moved along he remembered Sarah's reaction when he told her the whole story about the squaw's clay, and about the size of the wall of gold. She had been as excited about it as he had and urged them onward.

But now Jim knew everything else might depend on how careful they were during the few miles ahead. This must be the heart of the good hunting country. An Indian might be coming back loaded down with a ten-point deer. Or one might have been late making a kill, and waiting until new light to bring in the venison. A hundred different, insignificant factors were here, and any one of them might be all it would take to give them away, to expose them to the tough-minded Chiricahuas. If they were caught, they were dead.

The moon had grown during the trip, and now Jim saw that it was nearly half-full, and gave enough light for cautious travel yet without so much moonshine that they could be spotted over a long distance. Jim wanted to get out of that valley as soon as he could. When he checked the ridgeline he saw it was the same series, the ones working up toward the high saddle between the Sheep Horn Peaks.

Jim pointed up the slope. Sarah saw his motion and nodded. They began working

156

forward and moved a hundred yards up the slope when Jim saw a bush ahead of him shaking. There was no time to think through what to do. As with most men of action, Jim knew instinctively what was best and acted before he had a chance to think. He kicked Hamlet forward directly into the four-foot-high bush. As the big horse met it, Jim felt Hamlet's thick chest bump into something solid, then he was past it, wheeling the big mount around. Jim saw something move, an Indian, a kid! He rode after the figure, jumped off and grabbed him, slamming him to the ground. Jim's knife was out and touching the Indian's side. Then Jim saw the clay pot and the squaw berries in it. That was woman's work.

He pulled up his prisoner and rolled him over, and saw it was a young squaw, a Chiricahua no more than eighteen with hatred in her dark eyes. She glared at the white-eye and said something in her own language Jim didn't understand.

Sarah rode up, squinting into the darkness. When she saw the girl she frowned, knowing it meant trouble. Sarah dismounted and walked up. 'Oh, Jim, it's a woman. Is she with the hunting camp?'

'My guess,' Jim said. She looked too young to be out working on berries this time of night. Jim wondered why? A punishment maybe, by an older squaw? She was pretty, with thick

157

black hair tied back out of her way. Now she lay on the ground, pinned there by Jim's knee in her stomach. He held one of her hands so she couldn't hit him.

'She was picking something, Jim. Do they eat these?'

'Squaw berries. Never known what else to call them. I don't think you'd like the taste.' Jim turned to look at the pot where it had fallen.

'Look out, Jim,' Sarah called softly.

Jim turned in time to see her small knife flash down in the squaw's other hand. He jerked his arm away, but not before she cut a slash an inch long and a quarter of an inch to the bone on top of his left arm.

Jim swung his right hand hard, backhanding her across the face, rolling her head to one side. Jim knocked the knife away and pushed her over on her stomach, put his knees in the middle of her back, and grabbed both her wrists in his right hand.

Sarah moved up without a word. She brought a scarf from her saddle bag, folded the end making a pad, pressed the thick part directly over the bleeding slices on his arm, and wrapped it tightly with the rest of the long silk scarf. Then she tore the end in half and neatly tied the cloth around his arm.

'The blood won't come out of that,' Jim said.

'I know.' She pointed to the Chiricahua woman. 'More important, what are we going

158

to do with her?'

Jim sat on the squaw's back and let her squirm under him.

'We've got three choices. One, we can let her go. She'll run all the way back to that camp and we'll have ten braves hunting us down like rabbits within an hour. Ten of them can't possibly miss finding us and killing us.'

Sarah shook her head.

'Two, we can tie her up and carry her over the saddle until we get far enough out of her country to let her go, hoping that we have enough time to get away before she brings back half the Apache nation howling after our scalps.'

'The third choice?'

Jim looked at Sarah. 'The third one is that right here, right now, we kill this squaw.'

CHAPTER FOURTEEN

Sarah's mouth fell open. She gasped, and her eyes went wide. 'Oh . . . Oh, Jim, no! We'll have to take her with us. I could never . . . I mean just the idea of . . . of doing that to her. You can't!'

'Sarah, we'd never make it if Hamlet had to carry me and the girl, too. And she couldn't ride double with you. What it comes down to is her life, or ours.'

'Jim, I'd rather take a chance, try to outrun

159

them. If we get a good start, leave her tied up or something...'

'Sarah, you can't outrun a smoke signal. They would smoke talk to every Apache in the Southwest about us and the redskins would close in around here tight as a preacher's pocketbook.' Jim reached for his knife and Sarah's eyes widened. This time she charged straight ahead. Jim had his knees on the Indian girl's back now and he looked away from Sarah at just the wrong time. She surprised him when she hit his shoulder and spun him sideways onto the ground beyond the Indian. Sarah jumped on his back and began pounding him. The squaw sprang up and saw Jim's leg near her with the revolver tied down on it. She grabbed the gun and slid it out of the leather before Jim felt it. His lunge at her was an inch too short.

The squaw girl ran a dozen steps, then turned and pointed the gun at Jim.

He came to his feet, pushing Sarah gently down and out of the line of fire.

'Easy, now, Sarah. Just sit there. She doesn't know how to use the iron. An old squaw might, but not this one. 'Course she might find out, and just one shot from that gun and we're both hanging head down in that hunting camp.' Jim watched the Indian girl. She glanced behind her, saw the horses, and lifted the black's reins over its head. Then she slapped the horse's flank. The black snorted and ran a few yards

160

away. Jim edged toward her.

The squaw girl brought up the gun and Jim saw she didn't have her finger around the trigger. But just by dropping it, the blamed thing might go off, and Jim didn't want that. He never carried a round under the hammer, so that shouldn't happen, but the cylinder might have been turned already, or she might have pulled the trigger once when she snatched it. It was a chance he didn't want to take.

He walked toward her and he saw her move her finger, pulling against the housing in back of the trigger. So she did know a little about guns. Jim began to sweat. He watched in anger and a cold, sudden fear as her finger found the trigger. He stopped moving. She held the gun with both hands now, not used to the two-and-a-half pounds of dead weight. Jim swore at himself for not watching Sarah closer. He should have known she would react violently to killing the squaw. The hell of it was, the squaw didn't have to hit anything with a shot. Just one round blasted anywhere would do the damage. Jim reached slowly to his left side and slid the Case knife out of leather and moved it behind his right hip. Automatically he took the sharp tip of the blade in his fingers for a full turn throw. The Chiricahua girl looked at Hamlet, and Jim tensed.

Six feet behind him Sarah whimpered. 'No, Jim, you can't!' Her voice was soft, yet he heard her and hesitated. The squaw looked back at

161

him and her finger started to tighten on the trigger.

Jim knew he could wait no longer. He whipped his right arm from behind him in an underhanded pitch, spinning the big blade once. Instinctively he had aimed for her heart. He missed. The knife came at her point first and drove into her chest just below the sternum and to the right beside the downward curve of her ribs. The blade, nearly two-and-a-half inches wide, sliced through her esophagus, and completely severed the aorta.

Her face crumpled. A small cry came from her lips and the heavy Centennial New Model army revolver 1860 Colt slipped from her hands and fell. Jim held his breath as it hit the soft mulch of the pine woods floor. It didn't go off. For a moment he was afraid she had pulled the trigger as she let go of it.

Behind him, Sarah sobbed softly.

The Indian girl dropped to her knees, then tumbled sideways. Blood gushed from her mouth and she coughed once, then he heard the death rattle as the last of the air and blood rushed from her lungs and mouth.

Jim went to Sarah, sat down beside her, and took her in his arms. He rocked her like a baby, trying to sooth her, to quiet her crying. She sobbed another few minutes, then looked up at him and began crying again.

There was nothing he could say. She knew it was the girl or them. Jim didn't worry about

162

whether he would have been able simply to execute her, murder her without giving her a chance. But she had her chance, and a good one. If she'd known just a little more about guns it would have been the other way around. He calmed Sarah the best he could, then he went to the Indian girl. After cleaning his knife he put it away and spent the next fifteen minutes clawing out a shallow grave for the body. When he rolled her into it, the pit wasn't deep enough, so he piled mulch and dirt on top of the body, then dragged up a rotting pine log and placed it over the mound. That should keep the coyotes away from it for at least two days. By then they should be a long way off. Jim scattered the squaw berries from the pot, and dug another hole and buried the clay dish. When he got back to Sarah she was sitting up, wiping the tears away.

She looked at him, but she didn't say a word as he helped her on the black. They rode silently, Jim more careful now, and they moved slower, checking, watching, making sure of cover from one point to the next.

All the rest of the night they rode forward, up ridges, past narrow valleys, always upward, climbing from one level to the next, with the shadow of the great twin peaks ahead of them. Sarah still had not spoken a word since the squaw died. He was willing to wait for her to voice what was on her mind. He was glad she was waiting, because right then he had a full-

163

time job trying to get them both as far away from the danger zone of that hunters' camp as quickly as possible.

He figured they had covered almost twelve miles by the time the streaks of dawn began ripping open the black veil in the east. He found a small brushy spot and worked in behind it. At that point a sheer cliff wall came right down to the brush. By cutting a little of the growth, Jim fashioned an area large enough for the horses and the two of them. He took the rabbit he had killed the previous morning from his saddlebag. It was a little rank, but his nose said it hadn't turned bad. With the full light to hide the flames, Jim built a smokeless cooking fire. He had some trouble now finding small sticks and branches dry enough so they would burn cleanly with little smoke. This time he roasted the rabbit whole, turning it slowly on forked sticks and a green wood skewer. The fire at last gave off a thin blue haze and Jim worried about the smoke for the last five minutes until the rabbit was golden brown. He had roasted it at the side of the flames where he got the heat but not the soot. He cut the rabbit in half and gave one piece to Sarah. She took it without a word.

'Sarah, we've got to talk this out. I'm not angry with you about what took place back there with the Indian girl. What happened is over. You reacted the way you had been trained to do. I acted the way I had to. The

164

important thing is we got out of it without getting killed. Right now isn't the time to try to figure out if we did right or wrong. Now is the time to concentrate on getting through the hostile country and out the other side still with our scalplocks in place. Do you understand what I'm saying?'

Sarah put down the meat and looked up at Jim. She moved closer to him on the blanket, then fell into his arms sobbing. She cried, letting the tears wash away the last of the shock, the pain of seeing the girl die, and knowing that she had been the cause of it all.

He held her tightly, smoothing back her brown hair. Jim tried to talk to her, comfort her, but he couldn't think of any of the right words.

When she finally stopped crying, he dabbed at the last of her tears, and she let him. 'Jim, you have the best crying shoulder I've ever found. I ... It was quite a ... I mean, do you realize that today I've seen you kill three human beings. Three!' She gave a little wave of her hand and hurried on. 'Not that I'm saying it was wrong. It's just that I'm not used to this. Once Daddy was taking us up to his new command when the wagon and our escort were jumped by Indians. I shot at the whooping, riding Indians when Daddy told me to, but I didn't hit any of them. I saw some men die that day, too. But this ...' She shivered, then closed her eyes and gave a deep sigh. 'I know, the old

165

argument about it was either her life or ours, I know. The army uses it all the time. I still don't have to like it. I guess I've about used up my quota of talk for a minute or two. But it seems to me right now it's better to keep talking than weeping, so I'm talking.'

When she stopped she took a big bite of the rabbit, got the salt from her saddlebag and began eating. She didn't stop until her half of the critter was picked clean. They both had coffee as they ate the rabbit, and Jim wished they were in Colorado or the Sierra Nevadas of California where they could find some huckleberries or wild blackberries for dessert.

He went back over the details of the trail the old Indian had made him memorize. He had it so far, the twin peaks of the Sheep Horns were almost directly ahead of them now. Even during the day the weather was cooler, and he guessed they were over five thousand feet high at this point and still climbing.

They decided to take watches of four hours each so the camp would have some protection. Jim took the first watch, which he considered the hardest. He would keep awake until the sun was overhead, then wake Sarah.

She approved of the plan, then lay on her blanket, dropping off to sleep almost at once, her knees curled up, her arm under her head. She looked more like she was thirteen than a widow, Jim thought.

The day slid by without incident, and they

rode again without eating, thinking as much now about food as they did about the Indians.

Jim went over the map in his mind. About midnight they rode up to a gentle pass that lay between the twin peaks they had hunted for so long. Somewhere ahead now lay the valley of three fingers. They rested a few minutes. Jim considered his mental map again, then they rode on through the pass by the pale moonlight and surveyed the land below. Indeed there were four rugged finger ridges extending downward from the pass; creating three valleys. They had found it, the valley of three fingers!

Jim picked the ridge farthest to his right, and set a course down it that would lead them gently into the valley. They made it only half way down to the valley when daylight overtook them. As they made camp near a little stream, Sarah asked if she could wash up a little, and Jim said sure. He wanted to do some hunting while it was just coming light. But Jim knew Sarah was hungry. He broke another arrow when he shot at a rabbit he missed. Now he had but one arrow left. He kicked a rock on his way back, then paused, the idea coming suddenly. He used the bow and began turning over big stones. On the seventh one he found what he wanted, a three-foot-long rattlesnake. Jim prodded it until it struck at the bow, then reluctantly crawled out into the grass. Jim pressed down the bow holding the snake's head to the ground and with the Case he chopped the head off. The body squirmed and thrashed around for two minutes before all of the dying muscle spasms were over. Then he cut off the seven rattles and threw them into the bush.

Jim hurried back to the camp. He stripped out the good meat from the fat snake with his knife and put it in Sarah's pot to cook. The skin and inedible parts of the snake he collected and threw into the brush so Sarah wouldn't see them.

By the time she came back, drying her wet hair on her towel, Jim had the fire going and the pot steaming. He put the top on it so it would boil faster at this high altitude.

'Food?'

'Right, could I borrow your soap?'

She tossed it at him, then handed him the towel. 'Lay it out in the sun, and it'll dry in a few minutes.'

He went to the creek and washed quickly, and came back just in time to see Sarah peeking inside the cook pot.

'That's not a rabbit,' she said.

'True.'

'What is it?'

'I'll let you tell me after you've eaten. It's a little game. I'm on first watch. I'll call you when the meat's done.'

Over an hour later he roused her and they ate. She divided the meat onto the two tin plates and gave him a fork. Her first bite was small, tentative. She frowned, then lifted her brows and took another nibble. 'It tastes something like squirrel, but not quite. Is it coyote? I've never eaten coyote, but right now I'm hungry enough to eat almost anything.' She had another forkful and chewed it thoughtfully. 'No, this isn't squirrel, is it?'

Jim had finished his half of the meat and watched her now with growing amusement.

'I was going to say grouse, but I don't think they live here. No bones anyway, so it can't be turkey or quail. Is it some bird?'

'Nope.'

He waited until she had eaten most of it, then asked her if she really wanted to know.

'Of course I want to know what I ate.'

'In some areas it's a great delicacy. Texans especially like it. What you're eating is steak, rattlesnake steak.'

Sarah gagged, then gasped. Her eyes shut tightly and he thought she was going to spit out the mouthful. Then she swallowed it and scowled. 'You should have told me first.'

'Then you wouldn't have eaten, and you need all the energy you can get. It's really good meat. I've eaten dozens of them, especially when there isn't anything else. I stayed alive on rattlers once for over a week.'

Jim had put out the fire before they ate. Now he heaped more dirt on it and wet the whole thing down with a canteen of water, to be sure it was dead.

'If you're through eating, get back to sleep. You've got only three hours before your watch comes up.'

She finished the last of the rattlesnake meat, washed it down with coffee, and then cleaned forks, plates and pot in the creek sand before she packed it all away in the saddlebags.

It was an unspoken rule: they kept prepared to ride at all times. Nothing was left to later. Sarah lay on her blanket.

'Was that really rattlesnake?'

'Yep. I can show you the leavings if you want. Next one we eat I'll show you how to get the meat out. Could keep you from starving someday.'

She nodded. The strange part was she believed him. She wanted to know. She lay there watching him, wondering exactly what he was like when he wasn't in a life-and-death situation. Had he been married? When? What happened? Where was he going next? Would they get to Tombstone? She closed her eyes. A hundred questions ran through her mind about this Jim Steel, gold man.

*   *   *

That evening promptly at dusk they rode again. Jim was more confident now. The signs were showing where they were supposed to be. The lightning-struck pine, and now the glinting face of bare rock on the right side of the valley.

Farther down he counted six streams merging into one river and followed that one and he knew he was in the right one of the three valleys.

Before midnight they came to a spot where a ridge pushed a hundred yards into the flatness at nearly a right angle. He studied it, remembering. Yes! The slanting ridge to the right. Swift Hawk had been clear about that. They swung up to the right and rode along the ridge's bare top for two miles, then came to the mountain of no trees, as Swift Hawk called it. Jim saw why it could grow no trees. It had given birth to thousands of round white boulders, some small ones, some the size of a three-story hotel. Jim stared into the moonlight trying to find a particular boulder. They rode along the mountain for half a mile before he spotted it. A series of smaller boulders had been stacked on top of each other and cemented in place with adobe mud. The stack reached the height of two tall men and Jim knew he had found tall-man-rock.

Somewhere very close was the trail that would lead them down into the hidden valley of the wall of gold. Jim left Sarah at tall-man-rock and scouted ahead. It took him an hour to find the trail. He knew it was nearby and led to the north, but finding it was tougher. At last he spotted it, and rode back for Sarah. The trail was less than three hundred yards from the big rock. The start of the trail led through brush, and was entirely hidden from casual observation. You had to know it was there to find it.

Jim and Sarah rode onto the trail, and saw it was no more than a narrow ravine, that dropped downward quickly. The horses could walk down, but did a lot of sliding and slipping. By the time they got half way down the canyon, Jim saw that they could not make it all the way before dawn. He thought about waiting another day, then decided to push ahead. He would scout it out carefully with the field glasses so they didn't blunder into some Indian ceremony. They kept moving down as dawn came. Toward the bottom he saw the last sign Swift Hawk had given to him, a sheer cliff that faced east to greet the rising sun, and on top of the cliff, a twin-topped pine which grew more than a hundred feet in the air before it split into two tops spiring another fifty feet upward. Jim looked down the face of the cliff, but saw the lower half was masked by the edge of the arroyo.

'We're very close now,' he told her. 'Let's go on down and find it even if it does get light.'

'Oh, yes, let's go!'

They rode faster then, watching the streaks of dawn move into the black sky.

An hour later they rode onto the valley floor, and turned toward the huge cliff with the sentinel on top. Jim looked down the cliff now, and near the bottom he saw a bright spot.

Before he could tell Sarah, the sun broke over the ridgeline and a shaft of sunlight hit the wall, lighting it up like a giant, golden torch. Jim pointed, a note of elation and satisfaction creeping into his voice.

'There it is, Sarah, the Chiricahua wall of gold!'

CHAPTER FIFTEEN

Jim stared at the wall of gold in amazement. He hadn't been absolutely sure it existed until that moment. It was much larger than he guessed it would be. Swift Hawk had said it was taller than five braves and wider than five men holding their arms outstretched. Jim had been positive that was an exaggeration.

But even from a half mile away he could see the wall was at least thirty feet high and that wide. They rested under the shelter of some pines at the mouth of the trail ravine. Jim lifted the binoculars and checked the wall and the surrounding area, then the rest of the valley. He saw no sign of hostiles or any activity.

'Let's ride. We'll go up along this side of the creek, cut over in back along those alder-like trees and into the brush just above the wall.' Sarah nodded and they rode, galloping all the way in the open and pulling up inside the cover of the trees with the horses blowing. They dismounted and Jim led both nags well into thick brush so they couldn't be seen from the half-mile-long valley. He came back a few moments later and stared through the trees at the wall of gold.

'Can we get up closer?' Sarah asked, a strange new glint in her brown eyes.

'Couldn't be you're getting a touch of gold fever, could it, Sarah?'

She smiled. 'Guess so. Gold. I'd never thought much about it before. All that gold just for the taking!'

'If you can take it and still stay alive.' Jim lay in the grass on his belly staring at the wall through his glasses. They were a hundred yards from the *oro*. He looked over the ground carefully, paused at what looked like a pile of bones, and moved on. He saw no sign that Indians had been around for some time. Once more he checked what he could see of the downtrail, then the rest of the valley. He stood up and motioned to the girl. 'Let's take a quick look. Then we'll go back when it's dark.'

They walked in the trees along the stream as far as they could, then across the clearing. Jim saw where a landslide years ago, maybe centuries ago, had sheared off the cliff. A giant section of earth and rock had split along some giant vertical fault, and left exposed the wide vein of gold. As he came closer to the wall it looked like 'free' gold, which to Jim meant gold not mixed in quartz and rock of a deep mine.

174

The placer miners in California back in '49 took 'free' gold from the sand and gravel with their pans and sluice boxes.

Jim had never seen so much gold in his life. It looked nugget-pure to him. At the edge of the trees Jim took another good look up and down the valley with the binoculars, then at the trail coming down the ravine. Nothing moved.

They ran to the wall. Jim put his hands on it and felt the warmth of the sun. He pressed his thumbnail into the gold and found it dented easily. With the big blade he made a cut in it.

'This must be 99% pure gold,' he said. 'I've never seen anything like it before!' He tore his eyes away from the wall of gold and looked around the little clearing. There were the remains of several campfires. One looked like a Chiricahua ceremonial fire, edged with rocks. To one side lay three tall poles tied together at the top. They reminded him too much of another ceremonial fire. Then he remembered the bones he had seen. He ran toward the circle and almost stumbled over the bleached remains. Two skeletons lay scattered where the coyotes had left them. He picked up a skull and stared at it. The appearance was what he imagined it would be if someone exploded a cup of black powder inside a skull. It had erupted outward.

'They hung head-down,' Jim said out loud. Sarah had followed him, and heard his comment. She turned away. There was no way

175

to determine who the bodies had been. Jim guessed they weren't Chiricahua. They might have been a couple of braves from some raiding tribe, but more likely they were white-eyes. He dropped the skull and went back to the wall.

Absolutely fantastic! If he could get a team and a wagon in here he could haul out ... what about ten teams with wagons? He could take out enough gold to buy himself his own country; either that or he'd ruin the gold market. But this was a one-shot trip. Swift Hawk had not guaranteed their safety, but so far they had come out three, six, and even. He wondered how much gold the two horses could carry? They could fill the saddlebags, and put another twenty pounds in that canvas sack Sarah used for food. He went to the edge of the golden wall and saw how the metal flowed and melted into the hard rock. He wondered how long the vein had been exposed. Jim hacked a chunk of gold off the bottom of the wall, then scuffed dirt over the bright blade mark.

Looking at the gold he marveled at the purity, almost as if it had been through a smelter already.

Jim caught Sarah's hand and led her back toward the trees.

'Jim, I can't believe it. All that gold! Why, if we had a wagon? Wheeee, all the gold we could get...'

She looked up and they both laughed.

'Greed, is that a part of this gold fever too?'

'The most important symptom,' Jim said. 'At least that makes you normal. Everybody catches it, including thousands who've never even seen any of the yellow.'

Back in the dense thicket of brush, they set up camp, watered the horses, staked them in some lush grass, and then rolled out their blankets.

He looked at the cooking pot Sarah set out and preened back his mustache on both sides. 'Now I know how the forty-niners felt when they had to stop digging for gold to go out and scrounge for food so they wouldn't starve. Want to go rattlesnake hunting?'

She shook her head.

'Then you take the glasses and go out where you can see the valley and watch for Indians. They might be coming down here at any time. We don't want them to sneak up on us.'

He showed her how to adjust the eye-pieces and the focus. Jim took his bow and the one last arrow and faded into the V of the little gully behind them. There should be some game here, somewhere.

Before the sun was an hour in the sky, Jim returned with two rabbits. They skinned one and cooked it over a fire and ate it before it was quite done. It was delicious. The second one they saved.

Jim looked up suddenly as an owl hooted. It was unusual to hear an owl this time of the morning. He checked through the brush but found nothing out of place in the valley. Jim stared for a long time at the wall of gold. There must be a billion dollars worth of gold in there, a million-million! And he had found it! He wished he had brought in at least two pack mules with him.

Back at the little camp, he made sure the fire was totally dead, then stretched out on his blanket. Sarah moved over close and curled up against him.

'It's been so long since I could sleep near someone, do you mind?' She kissed him on the cheek when he turned, caught his hand and almost at once went to sleep.

Jim watched her. She was some girl, tougher than he had imagined. He bent and kissed her cheek and watched her smile in her sleep. Jim knew he should stand guard. He sat up a while listening. The birds were chattering as usual. Upstream he saw a rabbit take a quick drink and scamper back into the thick brush. By the time the sun was overhead, he lay down beside Sarah and slept.

It was dusk when he woke, and found the girl sitting beside him combing out her damp hair which she had washed in the stream. She used a fine bone comb.

'You snore, Jim Steel, did you know that?' she asked, watching him wake up.

'Only when I'm with a beautiful woman,' Jim said. He picked up the glasses, walked out of the brush, and took a long look toward the valley from the edge of the woods, but found nothing changed.

They had coffee for breakfast, and then Jim took the two saddlebags and Sarah's canvas sack and they went to the wall. He'd brought the short handled pick and now began digging out the gold, concentrating at the point where he decided the gold was the most pure. With the four-inch wide pick blade, he carved out a five-pound chunk of pure gold with every few strokes. Then he began cutting out smaller pieces to fill in the niches and chinks in the saddlebags.

It was hard work. He chopped away and Sarah fitted the golden chunks into the bags. Jim figured they could take about forty pounds in each saddle and another twenty in the canvas sack and still be able to ride the horses without killing them. A hundred pounds of gold ... it wasn't quite a ton like he went after before, but it would be a small fortune just the same. By midnight they had the work done.

They sat down and leaned against the most expensive wall in the world.

'Shall we leave right now, or get some more sleep and start out with first dark tomorrow?' he asked.

She looked into the blackness of the night. 'We've got water here and there must be lots of rabbits up there. Why don't we just relax and stay here a while? We've got some things to

179

talk about.'

Jim had a feeling she wanted to talk seriously about the two of them, and that scared him. He looked at the night sky, checking his Big Dipper timepiece. They could get six hours of good riding in, be out of this valley, off somewhere the other side of that ridge, and well away from this gold wall which he felt must be a magnet for some of the Apaches.

He was bending over the rough-cut surface now with his knife, trying to smooth the jagged cuts, to even it out so the loss wouldn't be so obvious. It was impossible. At last he cut off a piece of brush and dug its base into the dirt in front of the wall, so the leaves shielded the damage.

'No chance that we're going to stay here that long just for fun,' he said. 'We got what we came after. It's time we hightail it out of here before we get visitors. Don't really cotton to playing tag with the Chiricahua anymore if I can help it.'

They went back to the camp and put the saddlebags on the horses and got them ready to ride. They spent another ten minutes cleaning up the camp and obliterating all evidence that they had ever been there. Jim watered both the horses, dumped out their canteens, and filled them with fresh water before having a long drink himself from the swift-flowing, pure little stream.

Then they mounted and got to the edge of

the woods where Jim stopped and started to lift his binoculars. He didn't need them. He groaned and slapped the reins against his leg.

'Look, coming down the end of the trail to the ridge.'

Sarah looked where he pointed. At first she saw nothing—then the pinpoints of light stood out. Four, five, six of them.

'What is it, Jim?'

'Apaches. They're the only ones who'd show a light at night in this country. Must be coming here for some kind of special ceremony.'

'Can we get around them in the darkness?'

'Doubt it. They'll have a point man out, and side security too, I'd expect.'

'Then...'

'We pull back into the brush, up another hundred yards from where we were, and wipe out all of our boot marks around the wall.' He slid off Hamlet. 'You take the horses, I'll be along soon as I'm done.'

Jim slashed off a piece of brush and ran to the wall. He wiped out their tracks around the wall where there was only bare earth, then brushed out everything else he could see that would show they had been there. There was nothing he could do about the marks on the grass, or those along the stream up higher. He worked all the way back to the brush, and hoped he covered everything. When he was under cover of the trees, he paused and watched.

Soon a point man ran into the clearing, looked around, and gave a hoot owl call twice. In a few minutes two more Indians trotted in. The lead man hooted again, and five minutes later Jim saw the main group walk in, with pine pitch torches burning in the darkness. There were twelve braves in the party, and four of them carried a crude litter which held a body. A burial? The Chiricahuas didn't have any burial rituals he knew of. Once in a while an old chief was put in the ground along with his favorite horse.

As he watched, the braves leaned the body and litter up against the wall of gold and then built a fire in one of the former fire rings. Two braves stayed on guard while the rest rolled out blankets and lay down to sleep.

Jim moved like a soft shadow from tree to tree until he was well into the brush. Then he turned and walked carefully past their old camp to where Sarah stood with the horses. Jim carefully tied bandannas around the muzzles of the mounts so they couldn't whinny or make any sound. As he did he told Sarah about the Indians and what he thought they were up to.

'As near as I can tell they've come to bury some old chief near the wall of gold. Unusual, very strange for the Chiricahua. But when they do put away a chief, they keep it a secret. If they catch us here now, we're going to be dead in a rush.'

CHAPTER SIXTEEN

Sarah trembled at the thought of savages so near to her, so alive and menacing. She remembered how graphically Jim had told them about Becky's death at the hands of some of these same Indians! She reached for Jim's hand.

'Scared?'

She nodded.

'Good, we'll both live longer that way.' They worked silently, swiftly to build a good blind to hide the horses. Here they could use green boughs, small trees, anything to cover up the color of the animals, shielding them from downstream and the eyes of any wandering Indian. In a half-hour, Jim was satisfied with the construction. He put Sarah behind it with the mounts and worked his way toward the Indian camp through the brush with lead-scout caution. He had heard some chanting, and what passed in Apache for singing. By the time he got to the ragged edge of the heavy brush line where he could lie on his belly and peer under the growth, the old Indian chief was gone. Jim searched the surrounding area carefully, but couldn't find any evidence of a grave or a body. He counted the warriors: there were still twelve, which meant they all were around the fire. At once he saw the reason: A gourd passed from hand to hand, and each brave drank. As Jim watched the braves he decided they had already buried the leader and had disguised the grave so no one could find it.

The burial done, it was time to relax. Jim was sure they drank *tis-win*, a potent Chiricahua brew made of fermented cactus and berry juices. He remembered the time he had tried it and couldn't talk for an hour. Before daylight four of the Indians had passed out from the drink. Four others got ready to leave and, as they did, Jim saw that each had a strong bow and heavy, big-game-hunting tips on their arrows. He checked the other warriors with his binoculars and saw that all had the deer-hunting rigs. The four warriors took one last drink from the gourd, then hiked toward the trail out of the valley of *oro*.

Jim checked the rest of the savages. Those left were also part of the hunting team. And the first place they would hunt was straight up the creek, along the valley, and into the hidden horses.

Jim saw the gourd put away. Then the four braves who were still on their feet splashed cold creek water on the others, sobering them up quickly. Jim was thankful to the powerful *tis-win* that none of the braves had noticed the tracks or seen the spot on the wall of gold that had been damaged where he dug out the rich metal.

He was about ready to go back to the horses

when he heard an argument break out among the braves. He couldn't follow all of it, but made out a shouted word here and there. He got the idea that three of the braves wanted to wait until noon for their hunting. It was best then, they said.

At last they decided to wait until just after dawn when the big stag deer would come to the tender young grass and to the creek for water before bedding down. They would kill four big deer and carry them back to the main hunting camp.

Jim's frown deepened now. He realized that he had another two hours to plan what he and Sarah should do. Without the time it would have been simpler. Now he had to check out every possibility. Soundlessly, like an eagle coming into its nest, he worked his way back into the brush and upstream to the horses.

Jim told the girl what happened, then left. In ten minutes he had scouted the creek up to its three springs source. The water came from a crack in the wall, and above that was nothing but sheer basalt and granite cliffs. As far as he could see, there was only one route out of the valley. When he went back to the horse blind he told Sarah.

'So the only thing left for us to do is pull a classic cavalry mounted charge,' Sarah said. 'How fast can they run a half mile to the trail? We should be almost up before they get near it.' As she said it, Sarah took out her hand gun and began to reload the solid cartridges into the cylinder. She put in five, hesitated, then put in one more under the hammer, letting it down gently on the round.

Jim frowned as he watched her loading. He knew she was right. It was the same decision he had come to on his trip back downstream from the springs. There was no way to sneak around the hostiles, no chance to out-smart them. It had to be an old-fashioned, cold-steel, cavalry mounted charge. He was surprised that she had come up with the same notion, but thinking it through, he decided an army kid like her would have no other solution.

'When we do it is important,' he said. 'Four braves were so drunk on *tis-win* an hour ago they couldn't stand. But if we'd gone right then the braves on the trail wouldn't have been out of pistol-shot sound yet and they'd have come charging back. So now we wait as long as we can.'

Jim checked his own six-gun, slid a sixth round into the empty chamber, and put it back into leather.

'I'll make one more check on the Injuns. While I'm gone you look over the mounts, cinch them up, get them all ready to charge out of here. Right, Lieutenant?'

The girl laughed softly. 'For this you make me an officer and a gentleman?'

But he was gone before she saw his reaction. Jim moved through the darkness and the trees

186

like an Indian, never cracking a twig nor jarring the ground, never moving a tree branch.

When he got into position he saw the situation hadn't changed. Seven braves lay around the fire, drinking, eating from their pouches. Two were working on arrows. But where was the eighth brave? Jim checked what he could see with the glasses, but he couldn't find the man. He could be anywhere. Jim just hoped he wasn't downstream toward the trail. With the binoculars, Jim looked over the route they would ride out, even the top of the trail toward the mountain without trees, but he could see no torches in the blackness. The four braves who left before would be well past the treeless mountain now, and out of range to hear a gunshot.

Like a mist creeping over a wet valley, Jim moved back to the horses without a sound. He startled Sarah when he spoke to her, and he saw her hand move quickly toward her revolver, then stop.

'All ready?' she asked.

He nodded, looked over the saddles. Then he took out a plug of chewing tobacco and bit off a chew. He hadn't chewed in weeks, but right now he decided he wanted to. He had tied down the twenty-pound sack of raw gold behind his own saddle. Hamlet could carry it. He helped Sarah up on the black, then swung up on his own mount.

'We won't use the guns until we need to,' he said. 'We work as close as we can before they see us. As soon as they spot us we both fire once into them, and charge straight at them and over the fire before they can get to their bows.'

'And if we don't make it?'

'We'll make it, Sarah. We have to. Those are Chiricahuas out there. Apaches. Use your gun on them if I go down.'

'You won't, Jim. We'll get through.'

Jim moved up first to the edge of the heavier brush. It was almost dawn. Light began to touch the eastern sky. They were still twenty yards from the fire, and another six feet until they would be in the open. Jim motioned Sarah to come up on his left and they began walking the horses straight toward the fire. The creek was behind them. Nothing but a few stringy trees and a little brush now, then they were in plain sight. The light seemed to come faster until it was true dawn.

Both mounts still had their muzzles tied. He had told Sarah to jerk the cloth off the animal just as they began their charge.

They moved another five feet. Thirty-five feet from the seven hostiles now. A brave turned toward them, but stopped and looked away. Jim held his breath. He drew his six-gun and saw that Sarah had hers out too.

Five more precious feet slid under the big hooves. All at once it was daylight.

'*Eeeeeeeeeeeyyyyyyyyyaaaaaaaaahhhhhhhhh-*

iiiiiiiiieeeeeeeee!'

The Apache scream came suddenly. Jim pulled the bandanna off Hamlet's muzzle and booted him forward. His six-gun roared once, then again, and both the red men who had been working on their bows and arrows spun and flopped near the fire. He heard Sarah's gun fire, then together they charged the last dozen feet across the Indians, through the fire, and away. Jim felt the hooves on his mount slice into one brave. Three down, five to go. Both horses laboring then, stretching in the flat-out gallop that big-haunched quarter horses are so good at. They left the spate of trees and rushed downvalley. Then would come a curve to the right and on toward the opening of the trail up the cliff a half-mile ahead.

Jim glanced back and saw several bows up and arrows coming their way. But it would be a lucky hit if an arrow found any flesh at that range. He saw two red men running cross-country, trying to cut them off before they got to the trail. There was no possible chance for them against the quarter horses.

'*Aaaaaaaaaauuuuggggghhhhhhh!'* Jim screamed. He felt the hot searing pain in his right leg as it flopped out of the stirrup. Hamlet shied and Jim had no control over the leg to hold himself in the saddle. He threw up his hands as he left leather, and tried to ball up before he hit so he would roll. But the ground came up so fast and when he struck it that his

189

leg bent under him and another scream of pain ripped from his mouth.

When he stopped tumbling on the ground he reached for his .44, but the jolting fall had loosened it from its leather home and he was weaponless.

Ten yards ahead an Apache Chiricahua stood up from where he had hidden directly in front of the line of travel of the horses. The arrow had entered the front of Jim's leg. It had been the sudden movement of the Indian that had made Hamlet shy. Jim groaned and reached for his leg. The shaft of the arrow had broken off and now extended only an inch from his leg. He could see the twin barbed rear points of the arrowhead.

Jim looked up at the Indian and said 'brother' in Athabaskan, the language of the Chiricahua. The Indian hesitated.

Just then Sarah came charging back on her black. Jim hoped she would shoot the brave before he whirled and fired, but she rode past him, slid off the mount at Jim's feet, and knelt beside him, tears streaming down her sunburned cheeks.

'Oh, Jim, I'm so sorry. Is it bad? How can I help?'

'Start by shooting that brave,' Jim said softly. But she never reached for her gun.

The Chiricahua grabbed her and pulled the revolver from her holster, then pushed her down beside Jim. He caught both horses, and had all four of his captives well in hand by the time the first of the other braves ran up.

Jim heard enough Indian chatter to realize that his captor had been sent out to hunt for rabbits for a morning meal. The brave now had both the guns in his hands as well as the reins to the horses. He was grinning broadly. He let the other braves march Sarah and Jim back to the fire circle.

Sarah had to help Jim. The arrowhead worked out a little as he walked, but each step was painful. Jim put on an extra limp and groaned as he moved, then winked at Sarah when she looked up.

A half-hour later Jim lay near the fire ring, his hands tied with rawhide. They knew he wasn't going to run anywhere.

Jim sat up and called to the subchief, who he guessed was in command. He spoke in Spanish, hoping this man knew the tongue.

'Hunting-party chief, I am half Chiricahua blood. I demand to see Chief Cochise and deliver my message to him.'

The brave, who seemed a little older than the others, frowned. He probably was about thirty, but he looked like he could be fifty.

'You are white-eye who has violated the sacred wall of gold, and killed three Chiricahua braves. You must die, here, now.'

'You know of Chief Swift Hawk?'

Seven sets of eyes darted toward him.

'I know it is not permitted to mention the

name of a warrior once he has gone to the big sleep, but less than six suns ago I helped him to his promontory to sing his life-song. He told me of this place and granted me free passage from the Life-giver, so I may come, take the squaw's clay once, and then leave.'

'We know of no such talk. That warrior was very old, out of his head. You will die. Cochise has no time for white-eyes. He says all white-eyes in Apache land must die.'

'But I am half Chiricahua! My mother was Running Deer, she was captured by a white-eye rock scratcher.'

'Then we will kill only half of you, your upper white-eye half.'

Jim saw them build up the fire, and lift the teepee of three poles over the blaze.

'Even though I am only half Chiricahua, I am better fighter than you, old chief,' Jim spat out at the man.

The subchief turned, anger showing on his face.

'I am twice the knife fighter the chief is,' Jim went on. 'Do you allow your braves to do this hang-head-down game of squaws? Will the chief do the squaw dance around the blackened heads as well? Are you really only a chief of four Chiricahua squaws?'

CHAPTER SEVENTEEN

Jim watched as the chief grew more angry. The Indian did not allow a dozen suns to pass before he replied as he had been taught as a boy, and his fury showed through.

'I am subchief. The great Cochise himself set me to my tasks. No white-eye who falls from his horse can call me a squaw-chief!'

'Yet you cackle and crow in anger like a toothless old squaw. You cannot even hold your *tis-win*. You are not fit to be called a Chiricahua!' Jim turned his back on the chief, chewed his wad of tobacco, and spat a stream of juice into the sand.

He wasn't sure what to expect—a knife driven through his back, a club over his head, or a bullet from his own .44. But he had read the man's anger carefully. A moment later he felt a knife, but it was to cut the thongs binding his wrists behind his back.

Then his big Case fighting knife fell at his side.

'White-eye all talk,' the chief said. 'Now we see if *oro* thief can make his knife talk.'

Jim swept up the brown and white handle and struggled to his feet, favoring his right leg where the arrowhead protruded. A glance to his left showed that Sarah was not tied. The horses were still near her, still saddled as they

193

had been. The other four braves had not been sure of the Spanish conversation, but became instantly aware of the meaning of the dropped knife.

They formed a rough square around the two combatants, and Jim sensed a moment of triumph. The Chiricahua held personal valor and ability in high regard. If he could beat the chief, there was a good chance he and Sarah could ride out of the valley free and clear. It all depended how well his leg held together. He was sure the broad arrow head had not severed any major arteries, or he would be dead by now. It was bleeding, but not badly. He guessed that he could jerk the arrowhead out of his leg if he gave it a good pull. But that would come later.

Jim readied himself for the charge of the Apache. He held his left leg back, then jumped and skipped out of the way as the subchief moved in. He missed with his first lunge, then with a feint and a slash. Jim had to leap backward, and he felt the pain from his leg all the way up his spine. They exchanged feints then, and Jim saw that the Chiricahua was a master with a blade.

Jim tripped once when his right leg gave way, but he rolled and was on his feet so quickly the chief had no chance to drive in. Jim chewed vigorously on the tobacco, knowing he should spit it out so he could breathe more easily, but he held it. He hadn't had a chew for too long, and if this was his last one he wanted it to be a good one.

He realized that his right leg was more of a drawback than he had expected. He couldn't drive ahead, couldn't use it for leverage for a slash and withdraw. All he could do was slash and swing and wait for the Indian to come at him. It wasn't Jim's way of fighting.

He was glad for the heaviness of his blade, and twice he heard the metal ring as they clashed like swords of olden days.

Sweat dripped from Jim's nose. He brushed it away with his hand. His shirt was black with sweat now, as the older man moved in against him. The shirt gave Jim an idea, and quickly he unbuttoned it and pulled it off his back. Leaving his left sleeve in place, he wrapped the shirt around his wrist and forearm, using the padded arm as a shield against the Indian's thrusts. Twice he pushed aside slashes from the Indian, and found he could burst forward from his left leg stance and drive the Chiricahua back.

The second time Jim reversed his field and slashed forward with the blade. The eight inches of honed steel found a target, as the tip of the big knife sliced a furrow a quarter of an inch deep down the chief's right arm.

Jim moved back. He saw the beginnings of pain on the Apache's face, but he realized it only matched the throbbing pain in his leg.

The chief tossed the knife in the air and

caught it with his left hand, then moved in again. Now the chief respected the shielded arm, and each time it caught his blade he leaped back before Jim could attack.

For ten more minutes they stormed up and back across the grass, sand, and dirt of the little clearing, but neither could gain an advantage. At last the chief gave a sharp command and Jim saw two braves bring up their bows with arrows aimed at his heart.

'Enough,' the chief shouted. 'Drop your knife, white-eye, you fight well. You could not defeat us, but I see that you have the heart of a Chiricahua. You have won the right to endure a Chiricahua ordeal. Do you agree?'

'Which of the many Apache trials of manhood? The hanging flesh, the mountain sitting, or fighting a puma with only my knife?'

'None of these. Drop your knife.'

Jim did. It was better than taking an arrow through his chest.

'Which ordeal? As half Chiricahua I have a right to choose.'

Jim watched the braves. There was no chance to get away. The arrows wouldn't miss at this range. His hands were tied in front of him, then two braves took their bows and went running out into the hotness of the valley. What were they planning?

'White-eye, you have earned the ordeal of the snake. If you are truly Chiricahua, the snake will not strike.'

196

Jim felt his brows raise slightly and his eyes widen. He knew that he should not show fear, but these were reactions he could not control. He knew of the ordeal of the snake. It was a form of torture and sport among these savages, and no contestant emerged alive from it.

'Ordeal? That is no ordeal. You talk with the tongue of a snake. You are hiding behind the serpent, letting it do the job your dull knife and frail old legs could not do. Let's fight again with knives, with our teeth biting the ends of the same bandanna.'

'The white-eye is afraid?'

'Not of the squaw-chief, the one who squats to urinate like the other squaws!'

The chief surged forward onto his knees, his hand drew the knife from his belt, and for just a moment he almost stood. Then he settled down, put away the knife and laughed at Jim.

'The white-eye does not believe in the test of the snake? Does he not trust himself to the challenge?'

'A challenge yes, a real one, a true Chiricahua challenge. Everyone in the Territory knows the snake is only another Apache death torture, every Indian boy of six knows this. And all in Cochise's camp will know soon that this subchief, this squaw-chief, is too old and too weak to fight like a brave so he remains a squatting squaw.'

Jim sent a stream of brown tobacco juice toward the chief.

The Indian rose to his knees again, his black eyes burning with rage, but he slid down into the hot sand. He shouted to the other two braves who ran to the trees and soon returned with six sharpened stakes two inches thick and three feet long. With large rocks they drove three of the poles into the ground in a straight line two feet apart.

'Great white-eye snake charmer, you will lie in the sand next to the stakes,' the subchief said.

Jim did not move.

The two braves approached him warily, tied his ankles with rawhide. Then one of the braves rolled Jim onto his stomach, put his foot on Jim's calf, and bent his legs toward his back until Jim screamed in pain. Only then did the other brave cut loose Jim's hands and retie them behind his back.

When it was done they carried him to the stakes and pushed him against the three, placing him face downward. Then they drove three more stakes close against his body on the other side and tied him with braided rawhide ropes. Soon Jim was so firmly tied down that he could move only his head. He rested his chin on the sand, saving his strength. He knew what was coming.

Jim heard a shout from the two braves down the valley and soon one ran up holding a snake just behind its triangular head. It was a three-foot-long rattlesnake.

198

'Oh, Jim, no! They can't do that!' Sarah shouted. One of the braves slapped her across the mouth and she fell to her knees, sobbing as much from fear and anger as hurt. She stared at Jim, fury building in her soul. Why hadn't she shot that Indian from her horse when she had the chance? Stupid woman! Why couldn't she do something right? She could have tried to shoot him, at least. Now Jim was going to die, and then they would rape her and hang her head down the way they did Becky ... Sarah wanted to faint. If she had been in Philadelphia she would have. Now she dried her eyes and watched Jim, her mind furiously trying to figure out a way to aid him. The pistols were out of reach. No help there. She stood beside her black horse, but she would never have time to get on and ride away. What in the world could she do?

By this time she saw that another stake had been driven into the ground directly in front of Jim. The Indians measured carefully the distance to Jim's head, then lifted his head by his hair and measured again.

Jim understood what they were doing. He had heard about it first hand from a rock-scratching miner who was caught in Apache land and then was rescued before it was too late.

The rattler would be tied to the stake in front of Jim's face. It would be tied so it could coil and strike. But if Jim lifted his head up as high

199

as he could, the snake would not be able to reach him.

As soon as Jim tired, or as soon as the aching, cramping muscles in his neck gave out and his head dropped toward the sand, the rattler would strike and hit him, flooding his system with poison. The rattler would strike and strike until it was exhausted, even after its poison sacks had been emptied, and Jim would be dead in two hours.

Jim watched now as the final measurement was made by stretching out the snake and lifting his own head. He could feel the hot breath of the creature. Then the brave let go of Jim's hair and his chin dropped back onto the hot sand.

The snake was put down too, at the far side of the peg. It coiled and struck toward a nearby Indian foot, but the rawhide thong stopped it in time. The Indians howled with laughter.

Jim watched the rattler turn and eye him, its tar-black eyes locking on his as it slowly slithered through the sand toward him. As it came closer, Jim held up his head, straining his neck muscles. The reptile reached the limit of its movement by the rawhide and coils.

But it had to move back toward the stake to coil fully, as the rawhide restricted it. Jim saw the coil made, then the tail with five buttons on it lifted from the center and began to shake and rattle.

Jim had lowered his head momentarily as

the snake coiled, but now he lifted it again, his eyes staring at the creature as its head came back next to the spring-like coils. Jim lifted his head higher until the muscles in his neck stabbed with pain. He knew the rattler was ready to strike at any second. His life was on the line like it had never been before, both his and Sarah's. Jim lifted his head even more, just as he saw the lightning-fast blur of the triangular head darting toward his outthrust chin. In desperation Jim lunged backward against the rawhide. All he could do then was pray.

CHAPTER EIGHTEEN

The strike was short, Jim watched in fascination as the rattler jerked back its head ready to strike again. Jim tensed, and this time he felt the whoosh of air as the snake came within half an inch of his chin.

By this time Jim sensed the cords in his neck tighten. It was a strange, unusual position, unnatural. He became tired at once, and wanted to lower his head. But he knew he couldn't.

He looked down at the reptile again. It hesitated. An arrow tip jabbed the snake. It turned and struck at the arrow so quickly it knocked the wood from the Indian's hand. The braves cheered and laughed. But the next time they prodded the rattler, it struck at Jim. His head had slipped and he barely pulled it up in time, feeling the roughness of the snake's upper jaw as it grazed his chin. But the fangs missed.

Again and again the snake struck, and each time Jim surged back and upward against the rawhide holding him. Five, six, seven times the rattler tried. Jim's neck was one continual screaming pain now. He felt his neck muscles knot, cramp, his throat constricting. He had to beat it down, had to hang on!

'Does the white-eye still say he's half Chiricahua?' the subchief asked. 'My brother the snake seems to think you're all white-eye.'

The subchief's taunts didn't bother Jim. Not when he had a life-and-death problem staring him in the eye. How in hell was he going to get out of this?

Twice more the bullet-fast head of the rattler snapped toward Jim, twice more the rawhide held it fast to the stake and only a fraction of an inch away from a contact. Jim chewed frantically on the wad of tobacco in his mouth, the start of an idea forming in his mind. When the snake was prodded it opened its mouth and bluffed, its tongue darting as the rattle whirred. There might be a chance. He kept chewing. Gradually he worked up a big need to spit.

A brave touched the rattler with his bow, and the ugly mouth opened, tongue working. Jim lowered his chin a half-inch and spit. The stream of potent tobacco juice sailed two feet through the air and splattered dead center into the rattlesnake's open mouth. The snake jerked and slumped sideways, and Jim could see the coils relax. It slithered to the far side of the stake and Jim lowered his chin to the sand with a sigh.

A surprised cry of alarm went up from the Indians.

'Chewer of foul weed, you have frightened our pet,' the subchief said in Spanish. 'You have sent the burning juices of the tobacco weed into him. Now we'll have to find a new snake. But before we set it up you'll swallow your wad of filthy weed.'

Jim saw one brave run off to find another snake. At least that would give him some time to rest his neck. He consciously tried to relax his neck muscles, and at the same time tried to think of some way to outwit these savages.

Sarah knelt in the sand. She hadn't been able to watch much of it, but when the Indians kept prodding the snake to strike again and again, she was sure Jim hadn't been bitten yet. At last she watched and saw Jim spit the juice into the snake's open mouth. Now it was her turn to help. What could she do?

They had taken her gun. Did she have anything else? Her small folding knife lay in her saddlebag. When she had waited for Jim, she had put up her hair in a high bun so it would be out of the way. There were two four-inch hat pins holding it together.

She stretched and, as her hand came down past her head, caught one of the pins and pulled it out. She was still near her horse. They needed a diversion. Sarah stood and patted her horse's flank, then rammed the hat pin deep into the horse's flesh and jerked it out.

The black bellowed in protest and kicked out backward with both feet. The sharp hooves caught one of the braves in the chest and toppled him over backward. He groaned and screamed in pain as six ribs broke and smashed into his lungs. He coughed and wheezed a dozen breaths as he died. The black bellowed again, then bolted forward, running at full gallop down the valley.

The subchief looked up in surprise and anger, and sent one of the braves to chase the animal. He moved over and looked at the dying Indian. Now there were only three braves and the chief alive. Before the chief got to Sarah, the other brave standing near her moved up close. He carried both guns and scowled at her. Quicker than he could react, Sarah jammed the hat pin two inches into his bare stomach. He screamed and grabbed his belly, letting both revolvers drop to the ground. Sarah dove for the big .44 which was nearest to her. She caught it up and turned on her back just as the brave reached down for her. She squeezed the trigger and shot the Indian in the forehead from less than four inches away. He seemed to explode, then he jolted backward. He was dead before he hit the sand. She turned the .44 at the subchief.

'Untie him!' she shouted.

Jim translated the message into Spanish. The subchief moved cautiously. Sarah stood and walked near him, holding the big gun in both hands, aimed at him. The chief cut part of the bindings, then tried to stab Jim in the back with his blade. It slanted off the rawhide and before he could try again, Sarah shot him twice.

Both the big .44 slugs caught the Indian in the stomach, spinning him around and slamming him backward, unconscious and half-dead.

'Finish cutting me loose!' Jim screamed. He could see the brave who had run after the horse—and the one who had been looking for a snake—coming back now.

She used the knife, slicing the rawhide. As soon as she got one of his hands free, Jim did the rest. Then he grabbed his .44, pushed out the spent rounds, put in new ones, and caught Hamlet's reins. He swung up into the saddle, reached down, and pulled her up in front of him. Jim took one final look at the subchief. He was in no condition to draw a bow.

Jim turned and rode toward the one Indian he saw now. The man had left without his bow. Jim rode past him and saw the next brave near the creek with his bow drawn. Jim fired once, and then again. His second shot knocked down the Chiricahua, and Hamlet pounded past him down the valley where Jim saw the black. The horse was drinking at the stream. Jim caught him, watered Hamlet too, and helped Sarah up on the black. Then they both moved cautiously up the ravine toward the treeless mountain and out of the valley of gold. He double-checked and saw that it all happened so quickly that the Indians had not even unpacked the precious metal from the saddlebags.

When they got to the top of the ravine and went through the portal of brush, Jim turned southwest.

'We're on the far fringes of the Dragoon Mountains again,' he said. 'We should be running into fewer and fewer Chiricahua.'

Sarah hadn't said a word since she had killed the two Indians. He was afraid she might not talk for a while.

So Jim filled in the voids. 'Don't worry about smoke talk. It will take the one brave that's left half a day to climb up to some peak where he can get a fire going that will be seen. Even then the hostiles would have to be coming from behind us. We'll have a damn good lead on them before sundown. As soon as the sun goes down we'll just keep on traveling, all night.'

He stopped talking and dropped back beside her.

'Sarah, it's all over now. The bad part is all

over. Try to think how lucky we are that you made that black run away. How did you do that?'

But Mrs. Sarah West Edwards didn't say a word. She only looked at him with eyes that were still glazed in shock, with eyes that had seen too much violence for her to understand, that had seen her own hand kill. Eyes that were too sad yet to let her say anything.

The second day after their escape from the valley of gold, Sarah was her old self again. She huddled against Jim in the half-light of dawn just after they had stopped traveling and had built their blind in a lower-level desert arroyo. They finished eating the last of a rabbit Jim had knocked down with his knife, and now she was ready to go to sleep.

'You know, Jim, I never really understood about killing a person before. The officers and Father used to talk about it, saying, "If it's him or me, by God, it's gonna be him." Now I think I do see. When I saw you tied down there in front of that rattlesnake, suddenly I did understand. I knew I could kill one of them if I had the chance. Then my mind got to working and I made that chance.'

'You sure did. Did I thank you?'

She smiled.

'Looks like we're about evened up on this life saving business,' he said.

'No, Jim. I still owe you one or two more. Sorry that I blanked out there for a while afterwards. But I'm not used to killing other human beings. It was harder for me right afterwards than at the time. I guess because it happened so fast.'

He bent and kissed her soft cheek. 'Now get some sleep. I'll stand guard.'

'You were guard yesterday, and then you rode all night, and now you're going to do it again. You'll go to sleep on guard duty.'

'So court-martial me.'

She reached up and kissed his lips and smiled, before snuggling down against him and going to sleep.

*   *   *

Late the next evening they rode into Tombstone, and took rooms at the Arizona hotel. Sarah rushed to the telegraph office and sent word to her father in Tucson that she was fine. She had to tell him that Becky and Harry were dead.

Jim slept the clock around. On the following day he knocked on her door. She let him in and he was almost blinded. The sun shone in the window and hit the bed where she had laid out almost fifty pounds of raw gold.

'Isn't it beautiful?' she said. 'I've never seen anything so exciting!'

Jim noticed the new dress she wore and the new combs in her long, flowing hair. Then he showed her a sheet of paper. It was a letter of

208

credit to Jim Steel from the Territorial Bank of Tombstone for $15,164.34.

'Oh, Jim, you've deposited it already. It's a fortune, do you realize that. Most ranchhands work for thirty dollars a month and board and room. So it would take a cowboy over forty years to earn that much money!'

She jumped away from the gold and shook her head. 'No sir, Jim Steel. It just isn't fair. That gold is all yours. I can't take any of it. We've got plenty of money, Daddy and I. You saved my life at least a dozen times.'

'It's yours, we agreed on that last night. We split it. Make it your dowry.'

'Hey, good idea Jim, I'm not exactly a pauper, and if you'll marry me I'll give you fifteen thousand dollars I have, and all in gold!'

He laughed. 'You are crazy, you know that?'

She started to move the big chunks of gold off the bed and back into a black leather bag.

'No, I'm not joking. It would work, you and I, Jim. We're basically the same kind of people, and we like the same things. I think I've got the gold fever too, so I'll be wild to go along on your trips and ... everything.'

She had all the gold off the bed and sat on it, looking up at him. 'You think about it.' She reached for him and he bent down and kissed her. Sarah's arms went around his neck and she pulled him down on the bed, falling backward with him on top of her.

'Oh, Jim, you smell nice. You had a bath and

even shaved!'

'Yes 'um, guess I did.'

'I didn't even get to wash your back.' She laughed and kissed him again. 'Jim, I know you're on urgent business somewhere, but can't it wait for just a couple more days? I mean, if you aren't going to marry me, the least you can do is help me recuperate from my ordeal in the wilderness. The best way to do that is to just kind of *pretend* that we're married.'

Jim leaned up and watched her pert, round face and the just-washed long brown hair. She wasn't over five feet tall, but she was something special. What the hell, the silver deal probably wouldn't go through anyway. And he should see that she got her gold safely deposited. Jim stretched out on the bed and reached for the general's daughter, a faint smile crowding on to his suntanned face.

We hope you have enjoyed this Large Print book. Other Chivers Press or G.K. Hall Large Print books are available at your library or directly from the publishers. For more information about current and forthcoming titles, please call or write, without obligation, to:

Chivers Press Limited
Windsor Bridge Road
Bath BA2 3AX
England
Tel. (01225) 335336

OR

G.K. Hall
P.O. Box 159
Thorndike, ME 04986
USA
Tel. (800) 223–6121
(207) 948–2962
(in Maine and Canada, call collect)

All our Large Print titles are designed for easy reading, and all our books are made to last.